THE MONSTROUS FEMININE

DARK TALES OF DANGEROUS WOMEN

EDITED BY
CIN FERGUSON AND BROOS CAMPBELL

2019

THE MONSTROUS FEMININE:
DARK TALES OF DANGEROUS WOMEN

Edited by Cin Ferguson and Broos Campbell

ISBN: 1-7320946-9-1
ISBN-13: 978-1-7320946-9-7

Scary Dairy Press LLC
180 Middleton Mills Ln.
Palmyra, VA 22963
www.scarydairypress.com
Special discounts are available on quantity purchases by corporations, associations, educators, and others. For details, contact the publisher at the above listed address.

U.S. trade bookstores and wholesalers: Please contact Scary Dairy Press LLC at email: ScaryDairyPress@gmail.com
Cover art by Mario Zucarello

"The Monstrous Feminine is brilliant, unnerving, and deeply weird! BRAVA! Highly recommended for everyone who loves superior horror!"

—Jonathan Maberry, NY Times bestselling author of *V-WARS* and *GLIMPSE*

"In a compendium of ghastly tales that are as brilliant as they are depraved, Ferguson and Campbell have packed this anthology with fresh and worthy talents who prove, time and again, that doubting readers discount the female horror author at their peril."

—Moaner T. Lawrence, author of *Beholden* and *Bad Newes from New England*

"Maiden, mother, harlot, crone . . . creative power and destructive savagery . . . from purity to passion, protectiveness to revenge . . . womanhood is a jewel of many facets, and these fascinating stories by fierce and fearsome ladies examine both the sparkle and shadow of their impregnable depths."

—Christine Morgan, author of *Lakehouse Infernal*

"*The Monstrous Feminine* is more than an anthology of twisted tales and grotesque stories. It is a compilation of stories that shine brightly on the women of horror in a way that makes them impossible to ignore. The tales contained in these pages are brutal, honest, horrifying, and even scary, playing on the fears that everyone has. Some stories will leave you repulsed, others quaking in the dark. But every story will leave you breathless with the talent of the authors. Normally, when I review books, I like to find a favorite story or two. In this case, it proved impossible. Every story is unique, and every story deserves its due. This book is important, and the writers in this anthology deserve respect for mastering their craft, creepy as that craft may be."

—Scott A. Johnson, author of *Shy Grove: A Ghost Story*

DEDICATION

This book is dedicated to all women around the globe, and to the female aspects, dark and light, that live within all of us. From the intrinsic nature of creativity, creation and the X chromosome—right down to the mitochondrial DNA—we are humbled by all you do.

MONSTROUS CONTENTS

ACKNOWLEDGEMENTS

This anthology would not have been possible without the contributions of the wonderful women whose stories are enfolded within these pages. This body of work is the result of their collaborative effort where the authors were not solely authors, but members of a literary team who provided each other with support and inspiration every step of the way.

Many thanks to Broos Campbell, who tirelessly contributed his time and effort to editing this anthology. His keen eyes helped to make these stories the best they could be. And to Cin Ferguson, who spent many days and nights reading and re-reading these stories and providing developmental and line-by-line edits.

And to Seton Hill University's Writing Popular Fiction Masters of Fine Arts program which served as a solid foundation of learning, and to many of its professors and mentors who provided the rich soil of craftsmanship where each of these authors began to grow.

OUR PLEDGE

Ten percent of the revenue made from this book the first year of publication will go to The Global Fund for Women. Help us to champion women around the world! www.GlobalFundforWomen.org

INTRODUCTION

". . . the Female of Her Species is More Deadly than the Male."

In 1911, Rudyard Kipling's poem about close encounters of the feminine kind illustrates the dark and dangerous aspects that lurk in the shadow of every woman. Indeed, each human carries a dark side within them, but the exhibition of woman's more sinister nature has been highlighted in music, art, literature and history. It is mysterious and unknowable. It is the foundation of many legends and mythologies. And perhaps a reality exists there that bears uncovering and examination.

This anthology has fourteen stories written by very different authors focusing on the theme of "The Monstrous Feminine." In numerology, fourteen is the number that represents risktakers, ones who are never afraid of challenges, and is symbolic of individuals whose actions spread like the ripples on a still pond after a pebble is dropped into it. Each author has crafted her own story, digging down into her depths to pull out the dark side of womanhood to share with you. They invite you into their worlds with ardent anticipation and perhaps—just perhaps—you'll be caught in the mastery of their webs and never want to leave.

CIN FERGUSON
Virginia, October 2019

WELCOME HOME

by
Donna J. W. Munro

The birds had a half hour left in the oven. The pots of potatoes, perfectly softened to mash, sat in hot water, awaiting the beaters, butter, and milk. Sweetie wiped the counter three times, scrubbing away at imaginary gunk. There was nothing left to do. She'd have to go out there with the family.

The door loomed in her view, a sentry guarding her from them.

"Fuck." She dropped the towel, leaned her palms against the cold metal of the stainless sink and let her head hang, stretching out the moment as long as she could. "Fuck, fuck, fuck."

Grandma would never get over her baby using such language if she heard it and no one wanted Grandma upset. Uncle Frank's arm bandage seeped from an insult he'd paid for when they'd landed yesterday morning. There would be a scar. There were many scars.

Sweetie brought her fingers to her face, pressing her eyes until the color exploded behind her closed lids like a flashing kaleidoscope rising in the dark. She could imagine them in there, knew what they were doing. All of them lined up around the table waiting for their feast, knives and forks lined up like soldiers around large dinner plates. The family stared, waiting for her to entertain them. They might as well be waiting to eat her.

Savages, she thought, tossing the towel down on the granite island. Big clacking teeth and powdered faces.

The smell of arthritis ointment and peppermints hung like a cloud over their craggy mountain faces. She hated old people in general, but her elderly aunts, Uncle Frank, and Grandma made her dance this bullshit facade of being their loving heir. Their dutiful, caring Sweetie.

They'd touch her like they always did, pinching her plump, smooth forearms. Touching her pink cheeks. She knew even as she moved slowly toward the door, crinoline skirt swishing against the hose she wore at Grandma's urging. They'd touch her with their gnarled hands and sliding, papery skin lined with bulging blue veins because it helped them remember themselves before they gave themselves over to the family. When they were like her. She shuddered thinking about those touches and Uncle Frank's teeth, popping down as he talked. His eyebrows full of long wiry hairs that waved and peaked like horns.

There was no way to avoid it. She took a deep breath and pushed her way in to sit with them as the birds finished cooking.

There they were, lined up like decayed dolls around the oak dining table, like stern brown paneling framing their nodding white heads.

"Sweetie, come sit next to Granny." Her Aunt Rosie patted the highbacked chair between her and Grandma.

She slid past Aunt Liz, who reached out and patted her bum. Uncle Frank leered a toothy smile and lost control of his upper bridge, letting it clank down in his mouth, a clacking alligator grin. She sank into the gap between the women, letting them peck at her, fingers like birds dusting her chin, pulling a stray hair out, fluffing the fan of her skirt. They always fussed over her until it was time to eat.

She bit the inside of her mouth bloody, so she wouldn't scream.

Grandma clutched her with her arthritic claws. "I'm so glad we kept you, Sweetie."

She nodded at Grandma, blinking the water back in her eyes.

"We're starving," Uncle Frank said, hand skittering across the tabletop toward hers. She jerked her hand back to her lap, twisting it into her skirt. He hissed disappointment at her, but Aunt Liz tutted his impatience.

"The birds will be done soon."

She agreed, wishing that she could slip away from this rotten family. Run from them. Her inheritance didn't matter—money had once seemed more important than anything, especially the old life she'd sacrificed, so full of struggle and failure and freedom, but now… Now she knew what they did. What they were.

Grandmas fingers petted and pinched the fabric puffed around her. "You look so nice in that dress, Sweetie. I knew you would. Just like our little princess."

Aunt Rosie huffed, spit flying past her squared, false teeth. Teeth that hid the truth. "Why do you care what she wears? She's just as useful in her street clothes as she is in those frilly dresses you make her wear."

A low growl bubbled out of Grandma's throat, echoing in the corners of the room. Aunt Liz and Uncle Frank hissed and flattened themselves back, so that Aunt Rosie and Grandma could have words without any obstacles. Sweetie covered her ears against the noise and ducked her head down onto the table, knowing that Aunt Rosie's challenge would shatter glasses and rattle windows. Once they'd growled until she bled from both ears. Broke her eardrums that way.

She whimpered, waiting for the challenge to be over.

From the corner of her eye, she saw Grannie bare her teeth and lean in until Aunt Rosie shrunk back and ducked her head. The anger passed and the room's temperature dropped again. The challenge ended with Grandma tutting over the spotty shine on the silverware and Aunt Rosie agreeing that Sweetie should take more care when she polished.

"Stop it now," Aunt Liz said to her, pulling her up from her seat. Liz could be too rough sometimes, but Sweetie understood why. She was the youngest of them and had so much to prove. "Git. Go carve up the birds so we can all relax."

Sweetie nodded and hopped up, weaving through them, hands still on her ears just in case they started up again with their screeching challenges. She pushed through the door back into the kitchen and peeked into the glass window of the oven door. The thermometer she'd pressed into the biggest bird hovered at 155 degrees. Soon. Very soon. She hoped it would be enough for them.

She whipped the potatoes with milk and butter, spicing and spooning the mounds into a big bowl and setting it on the cart. Just meat and potatoes for her family. Really, they just wanted the meat.

With a sigh of resolve, she slipped her hands into the thick padded gloves and opened the oven. The birds, finally broiled to perfection, sizzled in the heavy cast-iron pots. One for each of them. Hunks of dripping meat tied to broken, hacked bones stewing in fatty pink juices. No matter how many times she did this, her gorge tried turning inside out as she pulled them from the rush of heat onto the metal service cart. The briny scent cloyed and wove through the potatoes' spice until it knotted into a delicious meaty cloud. Even though it nauseated her, it smelled so good at the same time. She hated that her stomach gurgled and begged for the meat, even with all she knew.

"Better hurry now, Sweetie!" one of the aunts called, though the voice melted and dripped until she wasn't sure exactly who it was.

The family lost their practiced control this close to broiled meat. With a deep breath and the first of the ten meat platters on her cart, she shoved her way into the dining room, gritting her teeth.

Finally, Sweetie had two weeks of blessed freedom. The relatives left as quick as they came, bellies round and satisfied, off to roost wherever the elderly went when they weren't tormenting their heirs. Without their watchful eyes, she let the house get dusty, wore sweats and ate junk food, watched Netflix in long binges, though none of it made her feel better. None of it mattered.

She felt like someone had pushed the pause button on her life. Like Grandma brought her life to a standstill. Two weeks of freedom, though their imminent return was a noose around her neck, pulling tighter each day.

She bought things with Grandma's credit card. Spent money like there was no end to it. The boxes from Amazon piled up next to the door, unopened. Things she'd thought might make her life better. Things that caught her eye. She'd have to hide them before the three weeks were gone, except all the hiding spots in the mansion were already full of things she'd bought and hidden months ago. Maybe she'd donate everything, just to get it out. She'd done it before, many times.

Her hair weighed down in clumps with grease. She smelled the three-day-old funk of her unwashed feet and armpits. Stink felt like rebellion, even if it was akin to the rebellion of a bratty child.

If she was someone's little kid acting up, it would be different. She wasn't. How many years reeled past as she did her time in the house? As bait. Sweetie didn't even know how old she was anymore, but compared to Grandma, she was a child. A useful bit of fluff. And Sweetie had chosen to be so. She'd paid to be here with her freedom, her ambition, and her real name—all gone to serve the family.

Sweetie was all she had now.

Two weeks passed and trash crouched in corners. Rumpled dresses ordered and sent by Grandma lay strewn on the floor, trampled by her restless feet walking back and forth across them like they were nothing.

She looked down at her clothes, so crusted that the logo on the front blended with the ridges of dried whatever food fell out of her mouth when the weeping began, and all her senses shut down. The things the family expected of her piled up as the weeks off passed.

Clean the house.

Buy the trimmings.

Dry clean her fourth-week wardrobe.

Select the meat.

That's where it all broke down for her. No amount of hours prepared her for the hunt.

Or the kill.

Or the feast.

She let a ragged sigh rip through her windpipe and hitch into a sob. Scabby, bitten lips trembled as her tears washed tracks down her filthy face.

She glanced at the door. Normal people left. They walked through doors and left when things didn't work for them. They fought against family ties that hurt them. They divorced and fought and broke away. But she couldn't. Her feet didn't belong to her. They were rooted in Grandma's dirt and tangled with the branches of aunties and uncles. Like the quaking aspens that stand all knotted together under the soil, they looked separate but were conjoined as a sinister growth that tied her to them. Consuming her life.

Consuming everything.

One week of freedom left. Sweetie pulled herself out of the couch. The cleaning crew expected this level of slop in the house, since they'd seen it all before. Two weeks' worth of hoarding and trash strewn in stinking, infested piles. Fruit flies clouded the air and Sweetie didn't even care what crunched under her feet. She moved through the trails she'd made in her filth, finally ready to tick items off her list.

The pressing, clenching worry wrenched her out of the mire she'd been in for two weeks. Gathering up the dresses wadded on the floor, she bundled them and her foul laundry into bags for the service and tossed them on the mansion's wide front porch for pickup. She'd throw away the outfit she wore now, not a big loss since it probably only clung together through the stubbornness of the gummy stains on the fabric.

The hourslong bath and shower she took used all the hot water twice. Sure, the water finally ran clear, but the filth remained on her as sure as the dried red wine on the sweats she'd stuffed in the trash. She'd asked the cleaners to knock on the door when they needed to clean the master bath, after they'd finished with the rest of the house. They'd swarmed in to clean the main areas of the house, and the hours of thumping and vacuuming and doors slamming couldn't go on forever.

Knock-knock.

"Miss, we will be to this room soon. Is that all right?"

"That's fine. Thank you," she said, voice flattened by the hours of tears cried into the bath water. "I'll be right out."

She dried herself on a soft towel and glanced at the mirror. Clean body, unmarred and as sexy as any model's in *Maxim* magazine or on the cover of *Playboy*. Not a dimple, not a pimple, not a ripple or a stretch mark.

That she hadn't put on a pound during her three weeks of freedom hurt her. No amount of bingeing stretched her or filled her. Grandma's gift to her, a gift that felt like another thing she didn't control.

She threw the towel in the trash and walked out of the bathroom, naked in the afternoon light slanting through the windows. The cleaners paused in their baseboard scrubbing to watch her walk by.

"I told you. She does it every time," one of the women whispered to another, openly staring.

What did she have to hide? She went into her room, not bothering to shut the door. The laundry service delivery man always hung her dresses in the closet and folded her underthings into neat little knots in the chest of drawers.

Her room sparkled with the fresh cleaning, sheets stretched tight on the bed and curtains thrown back, bathing the room in the bright light of midday. A beautiful fiction.

The maid's efforts would last for the rest of the third week, allowing her to hunt.

The closet's contents frilled and fluffed from one wall to another, organized by color and fit—a room of clothes as bright as macaw feathers. Sitting on a cushy lounge bench, she slid on silky panties chosen for her by Grandma, pulled thigh-high stockings up to the lacy garters and clipped them into place. Padding over to the mirror, she brushed her drying black hair into tumbling waves that framed her face and tickled her back with feather-like touches. Light foundation, a bit of blush, and some artful eyeshadow to add drama. Grandmother had taught her all thc tricks.

Then she pulled on a silver gown from the side of the closet full of "going out" clothes—shimmery, short, and slit to mid-thigh. She'd wear the Donna Reed flair skirts when the family arrived next week. She pulled on strappy black heels, not too high.

"You're not a whore," Grandma said inside her thoughts, a memory of so many conversations they'd had during her early years of hunting. "We don't want to attract the type that goes for that. Just be your beautiful self."

Her Porsche waited in the garage for her monthly club-hopping trips in the city. She strode past the last of the cleaning team, flipping her hair over her shoulder. She'd let the maid put away the groceries as they came. The crew would be gone by the time she got back, house perfect and provisions stocked. Grandma had brought her up for this. She'd given her everything, so she'd be the honey. The perfect flower, waving petals in a spring's fragrant wind.

In the car, she adjusted the mirror. Her eyes stared back at her, dead as a doll's. She revved the Porsche's engine, the satiny black paint absorbing all the light that skimmed its surface. The clutch gave. She slammed the gearshift into its slot, and fishtailed out of the garage's mouth, alive in the movement, loving the danger she made for herself alone.

The pink in her cheeks and quick, sipped breaths repulsed her. Why she did always bloom when she hunted?

Her Porsche rushed along the inky ribbon of road imprinted on the hills between the mansion and the city.

"Tonight, Manhattan." The sound of her own voice made her nauseous. It creaked across the words she hated to say. Sandpaper grit against the unhappy truth. She clenched her jaw and pressed the gas pedal down, speeding forward.

"This place is amazing!" Liza said, leaning against the curved banister of the wide staircase striped with the obligatory red-carpet runner. "What did you say your name was?"

"Just call me Sweetie." She stretched her hand out, letting her fingertips slide across the soft inner forearm of the beautiful blonde. How quickly they'd connected! Sweetie's buzzing call and vibrating musk attracted many admirers at the club, but only Liza, so full of vitality, drew Sweetie's interest. They'd danced together for a few hours, and when Sweetie asked, Liza agreed to come home with her with a trusting, lusty grin.

No one ever expects the beauty to be a beast.

She led her up the stairs to shower.

"Don't you want to … you know, together?" Liza asked.

"No, I want to make us drinks. I'll freshen up after you are done."

Liza's waifish body barely concealed her life spark. Her eyes seemed to catch fire with every glance. She strode over and wrapped her slight arms around Sweetie's hips, pulling her in to a warm embrace. Soft lips covered Sweetie's with moist kisses. The room swirled around her as their tongues touched and tumbled. She raised her shaking hands and pushed against Liza's shoulders, breaking the magnetic hold between them.

Liza panted as she leaned against the door frame. "You taste like sugar."

"Like honey," she said, then shooed Liza into the bathroom. Sweetie stood outside the door listening to Liza rummaging through the cabinets, touching all the surfaces, and finally stepping into the six-jet shower. The pulsating water striking flesh makes a particular pattering noise. She'd heard it so many times before.

Above Liza, sensors registered the use of the guest shower, the heat and humid air triggered their release of the payload they held. Grandma designed the system and explained it to her.

"Pellets." Grandma lifted the pill-shaped poisons into the compartment in the ceiling. Below, Uncle Frank started the shower so they could test the action as the mechanical delivery system released the pellet into the nozzle of the shower. "Just like the ones I designed for the Nazis. Clean and quick."

Even then she knew Grandma's past ought to stay there. Grandma's legacy in the world might be something whole libraries could be written about, but Sweetie didn't want to know even one more word. The weight of all of that death pressed on her chest.

"Listen … it hisses as it fills the room. Once you hear the body hit the floor, you start the timer. You can't open the door until the timer goes off. Fifteen minutes."

The meaty thump of Liza hitting the stone floor of the shower struck her like a fist. She gasped, unaware she'd been holding her breath. She pressed her thumb on the timer button, next to the light switch on the wall. The clock ticked, though it didn't measure time. It measured heartbeats. The scrapes and muffled thumps Sweetie heard through the door turned her stomach. Twenty-five years in the family business and she still sickened like she had the first time, so long ago.

Good thing Aunt Liz couldn't see her now.

Pressing her head against the door frame, Sweetie thought about how Aunt Liz earned back her name—her real name. She'd been the hunter for hundreds of years. Hundreds multiplied by full moons. Every third week of the month she'd hunted and every fourth she'd cooked. Sweetie didn't think she could make it to her inheritance.

Didn't know if she wanted to.

The timer dinged and she hit the button to vent the room. Her shirt, sodden with tears, clung to her chest. She still cried every time.

Only four nights left to fill the larder.

Sweetie opened the door, picked up Liza with her enhanced strength— a gift from Grandma. Then she carried her to the false cabinet, a body-sized dumbwaiter recessed into the wall. With a whir, the steel transport table pulled out and she laid Liza's body on the metal. Without that spark of life, Liza seemed so small. Almost a girl. The drawer glided back in and she pushed the button. The elevator carried Liza down into the kitchen freezer, an industrial cooler the size of most bedrooms, where the birdies waited to be cleaned.

She checked herself over in the mirror, touching up her lipstick and cleaning away the ruined foundation. Time for another club, maybe something in SoHo.

Day one of week four, Grandma landed on the roof with a thunk. Though Sweetie slept, exhausted from the four days of hunting, she felt them arrive like a tightening of her skin around her bones, squeezing her in a too-tight embrace. A trap with no escape.

Grandma made her way into the mansion, flanked by her brood: Aunt Rosie, Aunt Liz, and Uncle Frank. Sweetie squeezed her eyes shut and turned over, pulling the blankets up under her chin. They'd let her sleep, because she'd filled the larder. Five men, three women. Not a bad take.

They'd let her sleep because they believed she was too young to watch the butchering. That job fell to the next youngest, Aunt Liz, and someday it would be hers to do. Sweetie didn't want to see it, even if it was the next step in the family hierarchy.

She pulled the pillow over her face to muffle the thumping sounds. Sounds she felt in the tangle of thought between her and Grandma. Every cut, every wrenching motion, every single pull of skin from muscle assaulted her senses. But soon the tortures stopped.

Grandma made her way up the stairs. The rusty scent of the rendering, a misty cloak that wound around Grandma's shoulders, announcing her presence to Sweetie. She feigned sleep, but Grandma wasn't fooled. She never was.

The door creaked open and Grandma peeked her head around, white hair a ball of electrical current, her bleached cheeks so thin her skull shone diamond bright.

"Eight little birdies in the larder. Good job, Sweetie. Quite fine. We are all so proud of you," she said. "Sleep now. Tomorrow, we feast."

"Yes, Grandma." Sweetie sighed and burrowed further down into her nest. "Welcome home."

TRANSFORMATION

by
Sally Bosco

"I'm getting the fuck out of here, Stan. You're a fucking loser." With a cigarette dangling from her lips, Blair dragged her overstuffed Winnebago luggage toward the door. She brushed ash from the sleeve of her leather jacket.

"Have a nice visit with," I made air quotes, "the girls."

"What are you implying?" She purposely slammed her wheelie bag onto the carpet, narrowly missing the midcentury modern credenza. Then she bore down on me. Blair was a big woman. Not fat by any means, but muscular. Lord knows she didn't have to work for it. Some freak of genetics had gifted her with a rock-solid frame—a product of her Viking ancestry, probably.

The glowing tip of her cigarette dangled dangerously close to my eye as she towered over me. One of her long blond dreads tickled my nose and I stifled a sneeze.

"I meant, have a nice time in the Bahamas, dear."

"That's more like it. Now pick up that luggage for me, *Stanley.*" She always said my name in a condescending way.

As I bent to pick up her suitcase, she walloped me over the head with her studded purse.

The blow jolted me, more insulting than painful. I was a rodent to her, a bothersome roach. But one that paid her bills.

"See you around, sucker." Blair cackled like a demented witch and slammed the door as she left.

I wanted to follow her and give her a good slap, beat her up the way she did me, but instead I sunk down into our Danish Modern couch. Maybe someday I'd be rid of her for good. Maybe her plane would crash, or she'd get abducted like that famous case of the co-ed who never returned from the Bahamas. Nah, they'd give her back as soon as they discovered what a monster she was.

It was a relief to have her gone. Whether she was having a girl's vacation with her friends or meeting a lover, it hardly mattered. I was rid of her.

I went about my daily life. My job as an insurance adjuster gave me plenty of time to stew about things. Day after day I got up, drove to work, swiped my security badge, and then sat and lost myself in the intricate requirements of my job. I socialized with people as minimally as possible. On the way home I'd pick up some takeout: Chinese, Thai, or pizza as my mood dictated. Then I would sit at home and binge watch endless Netflix episodes, science fiction mostly. Throughout this time, I kept the place tidy and clean. I scrubbed the bathroom and polished the oak floors. In case Blair did return I didn't want her to think I'd turned into a wreck.

The days turned into weeks, and then months, and then I lost track of just how long Blair had been away, but the optimist in me hoped that she'd remain gone.

I thought maybe I was free of her. Maybe she had run off with a secret lover. Though I waited and anticipated it, there was no knock at my door. I was really free. I'd gotten rid of her. I'd pulled it off.

One night on the way home from work, on impulse, I stopped at the local pub. I didn't normally drink, but that night I sat down at the bar and had a Bud Light and talked with some of the guys. It felt great, like I no longer had to hide myself.

There was a guy there from work who came over and made conversation. He mostly complained about his girlfriend, but it was something. And a woman at the end of the bar gave me a smile. Maybe next time I'd say hello to her.

I went home late with the glow of a couple of drinks and the possibility of friendship.

But my celebration was premature. I entered the house and switched on the lights.

And there she was, sitting in the dark, waiting for me.

But wait. Something about her had changed. Her hair was shoulder length and flipped up at the ends, her makeup subtle and subdued. She stood and smoothed down the front of her powder-blue dress, which was cinched at the waist by a matching belt. White pumps with heels completed the outfit.

She had the appearance of being more petite somehow, and demure.

Blair rushed toward me. I braced for impact, but she surprised me with a tight hug and a kiss on the cheek. "Stan, I've missed you so much. Can you ever forgive me for running away?" She blinked her long eyelashes and gazed at me all misty.

I backed away from her and stared. Had she dug up a long-lost sister and sent her in Blair's place? Her strong floral scent—rose maybe—wafted through the air. Blair never wore perfume.

"What's the matter, sweetheart?" She stared with eyes that were too blue, almost electric.

I can only describe the effect as surreal. I pinched my arm hard to see if I was dreaming. I flinched at the pain. Dammit, this was real.

My heart pounded a conga in my chest, and I couldn't move. Something about her stiff-looking hair, her vacant gaze, terrified me. I considered making a break for the door, but I was frozen to the spot.

Her eyes opened even wider, like she had an idea. "I know. Let me make you some dinner." She smiled, but with an empty look in her eyes. "What would you like? What's your favorite dish?"

Blair would have known what I liked. "Don't you know?"

She cocked her head to one side like a confused cocker spaniel. "Turkey dinner?"

"No."

"Tuna casserole?"

Before she ran through her whole repertoire, I decided to tell her. "Lasagna," I said.

"Oh!" Her eyes brightened even more. "I can make that." She took geisha steps over to the refrigerator, opened it, bent at the waist and peered in. She turned to me, made an "O" face and put her hand to her mouth. "There's nothing in here. How can I make lasagna?" She paused, thinking. "We'll have to go to the store."

"Yeah. Sounds good." This could have been my way out. Drive her to the store and leave her there. Or just run.

We walked outside. Our house was isolated, with no close neighbors, but only a half-hour drive into town. It was early winter, and a light dusting of snow floated through the air and covered the ground. She wasn't wearing a coat, but she didn't look cold either.

By force of habit, I handed her the keys.

"Oh no, you drive."

I gave her a long glance. The old Blair would have insisted upon driving. She stood at the passenger door, and it look me a few seconds to figure out that she wanted me to open it for her, so I did. She primly slid into the passenger seat and folded her hands in her lap. A large blue purse that matched her outfit sat at her feet. It was the old-fashioned kind of purse—stiff plastic with a short strap and clasp. I hadn't noticed it before.

"Okay." I got in and we made the half-hour trek to the twenty-four-hour Save-Much store. As usual, I drove carefully, stopping at yellow lights and strictly adhering to the speed limit. I waited for Blair to yell at me to drive faster, but the reproach didn't come.

We pulled up to the nearly empty Save-Much parking lot. The lot held only two cars. They probably belonged to an employee and some guy with midnight munchies.

Blair clutched her big purse to her body, and we hurried inside.

A cashier with droopy eyelids gave us a casual glance. "Welcome to Save-Much," he said.

Blair snapped a shopping cart out of its row and swerved to the right down the dairy aisle.

I stood back from her and observed. She picked up a block of mozzarella. Her movements were odd and jerky—almost mechanical.

I ran through all of the possibilities of what was going on. A) Maybe she was being nice because she wanted to get back together. She'd gone off with some boyfriend and realized it was a mistake. No, that was crazy talk. B) Blair had found someone who looked like her and sent her in Blair's place. But why? To murder me and cash in on the insurance policy I had through work? It had cost only a couple of bucks a month to raise the double-indemnity amount to a cool million. When Blair and I were getting along, that seemed like a good idea. Now, not so much. C) Blair was putting on an act to get me off-kilter and she'd do away with me first chance she got, probably in my sleep. This last option seemed like the most likely scenario. It was also the most chilling.

I stood frozen to the spot as Blair made her way to the pasta aisle. The thought that she might be plotting to kill me, along with the frigid air of the store, shot a tremor through my body.

I searched for Blair, but the aisles were stacked with boxes on top of boxes to the point that it would have taken a contortionist to maneuver around them. Though no one seemed to be unloading them, one lone shelf stocker stepped out from behind a box and looked at me. "Sir, are you okay?"

My confused expression must have made me look like I was about to have a stroke, or that my brain was being eaten away by Alzheimer's.

"I'm fine," I said, trying to appear lucid and rational.

He looked me directly in the eyes. "Get away while you can," he whispered.

That sent another shock through my body, and I started to feel that dreamlike quality. "What?" I asked.

"You might feel better if you went to the can." He pointed. "It's back toward the right."

I shook my head to clear it. I had to get control of my overactive imagination. "I'm okay. Thanks."

I continued searching for Blair, but the boxes that blocked the aisles seemed to be multiplying until they formed a kind of maze that I had to crawl over or flatten myself out to squeeze through.

It grew colder in the store and the Muzak, which had been in the background and barely noticeable, was now deafening.

Finally, I found her, more by her strong rose scent than by sight, in the vegetable aisle. She was contemplating a stalk of broccoli. She glanced at me. "I know it's a little," she shrugged, "unconventional to put broccoli into lasagna, but . . . what do you think?"

I exhaled, relieved at her harmless suggestion. "It's fine. Go for it."

She smiled with her mouth, not her eyes, and placed the broccoli into the cart.

I stared at the cart in disbelief. It was overloaded with fruits, vegetables, canned goods, eggs and bread.

She caught me gaping at it. "It was mostly all on sale, and you have no food in your kitchen. How am I supposed to make you nourishing meals?" She blinked at me with pleading eyes that were bigger and bluer than before, like those women who make up their eyes to look like animé characters. They weren't like that a minute ago, were they?

I said nothing, and she pushed the cart up to the checkout counter then and stepped aside to let me unload it and pay.

The cashier snickered at me.

"What are you laughing at?" I asked.

"Oh, nothing. You okay, mister?"

"I'm fine. Just ring up my groceries." I scowled at him.

"Sure." He kept his eyes on the bar code scanner after that as I bagged.

Blair pushed the cart out to the car in the freezing cold. I blew into my hands to warm them. Why hadn't I remembered to bring gloves? Oh, I had a few other things on my mind.

As I loaded the groceries into the car, she stood clutching her big blue purse. Not that she looked cold. Rather, she gave the appearance of guarding something valuable.

The drive home proved uneventful. At home, Blair stood and watched me as I struggled to carry eighteen grocery bags into the house.

Once inside, I watched Blair as she put away the groceries. She took each item and sized it up as though performing a calculation of what it was and where it should go. No way the real Blair could have kept up an act like that.

As she made the lasagna she carefully measured the sauce and counted out the lasagna noodles. She painstakingly sautéed the broccoli before putting it into the lasagna.

The dreamlike quality of the evening enveloped me. I tried to gather my wits and sit patiently, not looking at my phone or checking messages. I knew I had to be on guard.

Finally, the oven dinged. She pulled out the bubbling lasagna with potholders and placed it on a trivet on the table. "We have to wait fifteen minutes," she said.

Blair sat and stared at the lasagna. At first, she stared at it like it was about to detonate, but then she kind of shut down with her eyes locked on the lasagna, like she'd gone into power-saver mode.

If only I had a friend I could call to come over, but I didn't have any friends. Blair was right. I was a loser. No, wrong. I didn't have any friends because she had controlled my every movement. Maybe if she'd stayed away, I could have made some friends of my own.

Then Blair roused. No alarm went off, but somehow she knew that fifteen minutes had passed. She cut the lasagna into squares and served it—one piece for her and one for me.

I took a bite, but the food was scalding hot and I had to dilute the heat by taking a big drink of water.

Blair loaded up her fork, put the food in her mouth, and chewed. She swallowed with a satisfied look on her face. Then she gave that same mouth-only smile.

"Nice weather we're having," she said.

The snow was falling down like gangbusters. It was probably burying the car by then, though I didn't want to turn my back on her to go look out the window. "It's snowing pretty hard out there."

She put her fork down and looked up brightly. "Yes! I love snow."

Blair hated snow with a passion.

She continued. "It's really piling up now. I bet we'll have a snow day tomorrow." She smiled, wrinkled her nose and gave a little shrug, like it was all so cute.

That weirded me out. Blair couldn't act like that even if she tried.

She stared at me, probably noticing that I hadn't eaten much. All of a sudden, I smelled cinnamon and pie dough, like in a bakery. "What's that?"

"While the lasagna was baking, I put an apple pie in the oven. Everybody loves apple pie."

I'd been watching her closely ever since we got home, and I never saw her making any kind of a pie. There hadn't been one in our groceries, either, like a frozen one you can bake.

The oven dinged. She removed the lasagna from the table and placed it on the kitchen counter. She cleared the rest of our dishes, then pulled the pie out of the oven with the same potholders she used for the lasagna and placed it on the trivet that was sitting on the table. "We have to wait fifteen minutes for the pie to cool."

Before she went into power-saver mode, I engaged her in conversation. "You never told me how your trip to the Bahamas was."

"It was wonderful. We spent hours on the beach and had those fancy drinks with umbrellas."

The real Blair would have been in a dark, smoky bar pounding down straight Maker's Mark bourbon. No fancy umbrellas for her.

"Did you go anywhere?"

"We stayed at that big hotel, Atlantis. It had everything. Pools, restaurants. It even had a huge aquarium."

This was the most she'd talked since she came back. "Did you tour the island or go into town?"

"Yes, we took a shuttle and went shopping. We ate some local food."

"What kind of food?"

She sat up straight and snapped her head slightly, like some kind of alarm registered in her head. "It's been fifteen minutes. Time to eat some pie." She cut us both thick slices.

The pie was molten, and again I had to wait for it to cool off while she sailed right into it.

Her large, blue plastic purse still sat at her feet. She made sure it was never very far from her. I couldn't help but wonder what was in it.

She finished eating in record time and glanced at my plate. "You haven't touched your pie." Her expression was one of alarm.

I held out my hand. "I'm good. Just full from that wonderful lasagna." I couldn't even force down two bites.

"I'll clean up then." She rose, went out to the kitchen and cleaned with utmost efficiency.

As she wiped the dishes, I gazed out the window. The snow was a quarter up the car, and there was no sign of snowplows. The roads would be dangerously slick.

Blair turned and stared at me with a gaze that was so vacant, so icy and soulless, it completely creeped me out. I thought of making an escape, but driving on the treacherous roads would be more dangerous then braving the night with the Blair-bot. So, I decided to stay up all night and watch her.

After she finished cleaning, she sat across from me in the living room, setting her big purse down by her seat. Still wearing her color-coordinated apron over her dress, she sat still and stared at me.

Just looking at her made my palms sweat. To cut the tension, I decided to talk to her again. "I've noticed that you're . . . different since you returned." That was an understatement.

She got up from her seat, sat next to me on the couch and took my hand in hers. "Stan, I'm so sorry for that little spat we had before I left." Her eyes misted over.

Something inside me softened. I stroked her warm, smooth hand. "It's okay."

"I value what we have so much that I wanted to make it up to you." Dammit, she looked sincere.

"Really?"

"Yes. I want to be the perfect wife. Maybe have a baby together."

"A baby?" Blair had thought that babies were the devil's spawn. She never would have agreed to give birth to one.

"Yes." She nodded and looked down into her lap all shy.

I didn't know what to think. Maybe it *was* Blair and she wanted a fresh start.

She gazed at me with soft eyes and drew her face close to mine. Then she kissed me. That sent off alarms in my brain. She intended to soften me up and then she'd kill me. I pushed her away and stood up.

"What's wrong, Stan?" She glanced up at me with big, pleading eyes.

The way she said my name was so sweet, almost reverent. It reminded me of the way Blair was when we were first dating. The Blair that liked walks through the forest and midnight reveries in the moonlight.

When her soft hand glanced the inside of my thigh, it set off feelings within me that I'd thought were completely gone. Then she kissed my hand and worked her way up to my lips. I let her pull me into the bedroom. When she grabbed her purse and took it with her, that should have been a red flag, but I chose to ignore it at the time.

Once in the bedroom, she unbuttoned her blouse, and any thoughts I might have had that she wasn't the real Blair were swept away. Her skin was so luscious, and her mouth tasted of apples. To tell the truth,

I got lost in her, and I found myself wishing that she'd stay—that the real Blair would stay away.

The love we made was so sweet, it was as though she knew exactly what I wanted, like she was reading my mind.

Soon after that I fell asleep. I must have been dreaming for some time, and then woke up in the middle of the night with a start. I checked my phone. Three AM exactly. The Blair-bot lay next to me. I'd been temporarily lulled by her sultry ways, but, more clearheaded now, I realized that there could be no mistaking her for the real Blair. And what did she have in that big blue purse of hers that she wouldn't let out of her sight?

I slid out of bed as quietly as I could, crept around to her side of the bed, and lifted her purse. On bare feet I tiptoed into the bathroom and locked the door carefully so there was no sound.

When I flipped on the light, I recoiled from the brightness, but once my eyes adjusted, I lay the big plastic purse on the vanity. I put a towel over the clasp to muffle the sound and snapped it open.

The blood drained from my head as I stared down at a shiny, gleaming dagger, six or seven inches long. I tested its sharpness by dragging my thumb across it. A thin, red line formed into a drop of blood on my skin. This thing was sharp as shit.

What to do? I made up my mind to grab my clothes, wallet, and car keys and get the fuck out of there. Even if the snowy roads presented a deathtrap, it was better than dealing with this monster.

I took the knife just in case and put the purse on the bathroom floor. All I could think of was getting out of there. As I opened the door and turned to leave I caught sight of something in the mirror—a flash of blue. My breath caught as I saw Blair standing there, fully clothed now in her powder-blue dress and heels.

The knife in my hand was hidden behind the partially opened door.

"What are you doing?" She said this in a flat monotone voice, almost a whisper. Yet her expression, the intensity of her eyes, and the hard set of her jaw betrayed her true intentions.

"Nothing, uh, just needed to go to the bathroom." My mouth formed into a painful smile.

Her glance drifted to the bathroom floor, and she asked with a scary quiet voice, "What are you doing with my purse?"

"Um, I, uh, think you left it there."

Her eyes flashed wide. "I did not leave it there."

My mind raced. I decided to turn the tables on her. "What were you doing with a knife in your purse? What were you going to do with it?"

She searched for an answer. "It's for self-protection."

"Uh, what do you need protecting from?"

"You." Her eyes narrowed.

"Me?" I couldn't fathom it.

"Yes. I saw the way you used to look at me, the hatred in your eyes. You would've done away with me if you could have, but you were too cowardly, too much of a loser to carry it through. That's why I went away. I was afraid of you."

I was halfway relieved to see the real Blair re-emerge, like some form of sanity returning to my life. At least it was an explanation of sorts for why she'd been acting so weird.

I still had the knife in my hand.

"Let me have it. Now!" she shouted. Her eyes blazed.

I backed away from her in the tiny bathroom. "Listen, we need to talk. We can make things right again. I'm sorry for everything I might have done."

"Oh, you're sorry. We can talk about that later, but first give me the knife."

She pushed the door open, sending me backwards, then she made a grab for the knife but just succeeded in cutting her hand.

"Blair, be reasonable."

As I talked, she grabbed for the handle, oblivious to the blood spurting from her cut hand, but I pushed her away. That worked until she let out an eardrum-shattering scream.

We were miles from anyone, and no one would have heard her. Still, her scream rattled me to the point that she was able to grab for the handle of the knife and take it from me.

"Let's see who's sorry now." She stabbed the knife toward my heart. I slid to the side, causing her to nick the skin on my naked stomach. I managed to grab her wrist and direct the knife away from me.

I aimed it toward her throat. "Listen, I don't want to do this."

She wrestled the knife back again and pointed it at my left eye.

By reflex, I grabbed her wrist and twisted the knife away.

"What kind of man are you that you can't even win a knife fight with a woman." She cackled that unmistakable laugh and wrenched the knife toward me again.

But I grabbed it, and with the force of shame I jabbed it in her direction.

. . . And nicked the left side of her throat. Blood spurted out. Her eyes went wide, and she pressed both hands against the wound as she staggered backwards.

I dropped the knife and it clattered to the tiles on the bathroom floor. I raced to the other room and called 911. "There's been an accident. I just stabbed my wife." I couldn't speak any more. The shock had been so great that I must have fainted.

The ambulance and police car pulled up to the house, and an officer knocked at the door. When there was no answer he tried the handle and, having no luck, pried open the door by using a Halligan bar, which functioned as a giant crowbar.

A figure in a blue dress and white pumps sat slumped in the living room chair. Blood drenched the chair and carpet.

One of the EMTs ran over to the figure. "No pulse. I'm afraid we're too late."

"Where's the husband who called?" Two police officers had joined them. "You check the house," one said. "I'll look around the back."

"Wait," the other said, "I think we have our answer here." He pulled off the smooth blond wig, revealing a man's hair and, on closer inspection, five o'clock shadow. "He must have tried to kill himself, then called us."

The EMT shook his head. "I'll never understand human nature."

Three days later a story in the *Riverwood Times* read:

Strange Occurrence in Riverwood Reveals Hidden Murder

When Riverwood EMTs responded to a 911 call, they had no idea that they would uncover a formerly unknown murder.

On November 28 at 3 AM, the Riverwood 911 office received a call from Mr. Stanley Mercer that he had accidentally stabbed his wife, Mrs. Blair Mercer.

When police and paramedics arrived, they found Mr. Mercer dressed in his wife's clothing, apparently having stabbed himself in the jugular vein.

He called 911 and sat down to wait for an ambulance, but bled to death before EMTs arrived. His wife was nowhere to be found.

A grocery receipt led the police to the Save-Much store in Riverdale, where a cashier reported he had seen Mr. Mercer in the store the night of his apparent suicide wearing a blue dress and blond wig.

It was determined that Mrs. Mercer had been missing for over three months, though no one had reported her missing. An investigation revealed she had been buried in a shallow grave at the back of the Mercer property on 144 King's Road. Pending a formal investigation, the Riverwood police indicated that Mr. Mercer is most likely guilty of the murder.

WAIF AND THE WENDIGO

by
Amber Bliss

The family vacation to the White Lodge ski resort in New Hampshire was supposed to be a big deal. Thanksgiving with the family, their first holiday together since Cecelia was hospitalized. Mark—who was not her real father—was determined to make the weeklong hiatus picture perfect.

For Cecelia, it had all the ingredients of a nightmare.

Mark drove the whole way while Katherine—who was her real mother—chattered incessantly about how the vacation away from the city was just what the family needed to come together after their rough patch. She was already two glasses of wine into her dream life, and *rough patch* held an accusatory lilt. Eating disorders weren't part of the dream, and when Cecelia's problem had gotten out of hand, a stint in the hospital and a rehab facility had shattered the precious family denial. It was all her fault they weren't normal. It was all her fault they weren't perfect.

Katherine adjusted her visor mirror to see into the back seat.

"Cecelia, really, couldn't you have at least tried to make yourself a little presentable? I got you that lovely under-eye concealer from Italy." She set her travel cup of vino down and snapped open her purse. Plastic cases and pill canisters clattered around as she dug out a stick of concealer and thrust her arm between the seats to present it.

Cecelia turned toward the window. After a moment, Katherine withdrew her arm with a huff. Cecelia did her best to ignore the parental hostility for her little brother's sake. Matthew was six, and the sweetest kid in the world. If she played her cards right and kept it together, in four years she would be eighteen. She could get Matty away from Mark and Katherine, before they broke him down and snuffed out his smile.

The White Lodge was a magazine cover without the gloss, all rustic charm and seamlessly incorporated technology. The wilderness retreat for those who could afford to take convenience with them.

The urge to vandalize the faux log walls with black paint and cheap posters had Cecelia twisting her long blond hair the second they stepped through the front doors. Mark strode ahead to the front desk.

Her mother swatted her hand. "Cece, stop it. You know Mark hates that."

She ground her teeth and took Matty's hand. Offending the all-powerful Mark in the sacred public eye was a grave sin, so she led her little brother to the gift shop full of tourist-quality native trinkets and key chains.

After they settled their things into their suite, they went to dinner on-site at the Red Wolf Bar and Grill. The food was typical steakhouse fare, served under the watchful gaze of what she hoped were synthetic mounted heads. Cecelia sat under the massive antlers of the buck looming above their table. The whole place gave her the creeps. She couldn't understand why anyone would want to eat with an unblinking audience of severed heads, but Mark loved it because Mark loved all of Mark's decisions, and her mother agreed because she agreed with all of Mark's decisions.

"How's your food, Matty?" Katherine asked.

Matty stirred a puddle of barbecue sauce with a fry, his focus fixed on his plate, and his soft features glum. "It's good."

"Look at your mother when you talk to her," Mark said.

Matty jerked his head up an inch and smiled. "It's really good, Mommy."

Mark and Katherine both turned their attention to Cecelia, and she squeezed her fork until her palm ached. Family meals were a time of silent judgment, where she was weighed by the amount of food left on her plate.

She put a tiny bite of steak in her mouth and chewed. The twenty-five-dollar cut of meat turned bland and stiff in her mouth. She swallowed it with ice water, like a bad medicine. Even with Mark and

Katherine's constant criticism, she did not want to go back to the hospital. She was trying to be better, trying to stay well, but it was hard when a full stomach felt so *wrong*. She'd been hungry for so long it was normal. Every meal, no matter how small, felt like a rock in her stomach, or worse, like it would destroy her.

Prozac helped with her anxiety, but the demons still nagged at the edge of her mind, still whispered that every bite she took would turn her into a useless, soft, flabby thing, make her weak. That feeling was wrong, it was only her illness, but on some nights she still thought she would rather be crazy than weak. Her mother was weak.

Cecelia forced down as much food as she could, and when they finally got back to their suite she went straight to bed, swollen and dejected. Her mother set her door ajar and left without a word. One of the provisions of her release was that she couldn't be alone for four hours after her meals. To discourage purging. She had to be supervised like a bad dog.

Cecelia turned away from the light of the common room toward the big, dark window by her bed. Snow swirled outside, illuminated only by moonlight glinting though the clouds now and then. The tall pines of the tree line stood like black sentinels, silent, still, strong, while her body throbbed around the hot knot in her gut. She checked the time again and again on her cell phone. Hours passed. The sounds of her family moving about died as time bled into the night, and the weight of sleep finally pressed down on her.

Something pale moved at the edge of the trees. Moonlight glowed on its crown of bone-white antlers. A buck? The tiny shape picked through the shadows and stopped. Heat rushed through Cecelia's body, and her heart thumped. It was too far to see clearly, but the creature seemed to stare right through her window. Her mouth went dry.

Its gleaming antlers drifted higher against the wooded backdrop. Too high, as if it floated. Or stood.

The family hit the slopes after an uncomfortable breakfast. They hadn't been a vacationing family until Mark came into the picture. It was always hiking, kayaking, zip-lining— something Mark could work himself up enough over to forget about his thinning hair. She missed not having vacations. Cecelia did a few passes down a couple of the bunny slopes while Mark and Katherine tried to teach Matty how to step with skis on, but when she saw the red on Mark's complexion darken from simple frost-pinked cheeks, she stopped to hover nearby.

Matty took another fall, bundled too tight in winter gear to right himself whenever his balance faltered. Tiny sobs interrupted his pants of effort.

Cecelia knelt to take her skis off.

Mark stormed over to him and hauled him to his feet by his arm. "Stop crying."

"Mark, honey—" Katherine began.

"Don't start. He needs to learn." He shook both of Matty's shoulders. "You need to stop crying and pay attention."

Matty's lips trembled with effort to hold back sobs. "But it's hard. I don't like skiing anymore." He sniffled. "I wanna go sledding."

"No. You're going to learn this and you're going to learn it the right way."

Fat tears rolled over Matty's pink cheeks.

Cecelia kicked her skis off and crunched over to them. "He doesn't want to ski. Leave him alone."

A hint of a snarl curled Mark's lips. "Cecelia, mind your own business. I'm the parent here."

No. He wasn't. Cecelia looked to Katherine. Her mother's pale face showed a cowed expression. She wasn't going to do anything. Not against her wonderful second husband. Not even for her own son.

Matty's fierce effort to hold back more tears broke with a sob.

"Stop crying like a baby and man up. You're six." Mark shook him again.

Fine. She'd stop it.

Cecelia grabbed Mark's arm, planted her hand on his face, and shoved him hard. She only weighed a hundred pounds soaking wet, but Mark's crouch was poorly balanced and he spilled onto his butt.

She clenched her fists. "Leave him alone and stop yelling at him! You're scaring him!"

The look of shock on the infallible Mark's face melted into a murderous stare.

Cecelia's heart pounded in her chest. The heat in her muscles urged her to flee, but she dug her heels into the snow and planted herself between Mark and her little brother. Fear and anger made it impossible to break eye contact with him. Even Matty's broken sobs and snotty sniffles silenced.

Mark lurched up in a rage and snatched the front of Cecelia's ski jacket. She flinched but kept her feet rooted.

"Mark," Katherine pleaded.

"You want to hit me?" Mark snarled. "You want to hit *me*? Go on. Right here." He tapped his cheek. "See how fast you end up back in a padded room like an animal."

Fear weakened her knees. She wanted him to hit her just so he'd let go and she could escape the hot cloud of his breath.

He was close enough to bite.

Her tremors stilled with a shock. The image hit her. She could lunge in and strip the flesh off his strong chin with a single bite. Her mouth watered.

"Mark! You're embarrassing us," Katherine snapped.

Mark held her stare for a moment longer. "Yeah. I didn't think so." He shoved her back and stormed away.

Katherine tucked her ski poles under her arm. "Why do you always have to antagonize him? All I wanted was one week together as a normal family. One week! And you can't even try?"

"Nice try. Normal isn't drunk by two in the afternoon, Katherine," Cecelia said.

Her mother's powdered cheeks flushed, and she gaped without words. She stormed toward them and knelt to remove Matty's skis.

"You can come and join us when you're ready to apologize and be a part of this family."

A small crowd now hung at the peripheries of their little family drama. If there was one thing Katherine hated, it was a blemish in the public eye.

"Oh, mother of the year over here for letting some dick shake and scream at your kid," Cecelia said.

"That's enough!" Katherine whirled away and marched up the slope toward the Lodge with Matty in tow. She held her shoulders squared and rigid, as if she felt every one of the strangers' long stares.

Matty glanced back at Cecelia, his big eyes dark and plaintive.

"I'll see you tonight, Matty." She tried to soften her expression to reassure him.

Cecelia watched until the distance reduced Katherine and her brother to tiny black dots on the white slopes, then she bundled up her skis and set off into the woods. She had to go back eventually. She couldn't leave her little brother alone with them, but first she had to walk off some of the hot fury burning in her limbs, and she had to get away from all of the prying eyes and critical frowns. She needed to be alone.

The straight timber pines muffled the sounds of the skiers, and after a few minutes of determined trudging Cecelia lost the sounds of humanity completely. The silence drowned out the harshness of judgment and ushered in the serenity of winter stillness. Her fury ebbed, but the image of Mark's furious face as he dared her to hit him fixated in her mind.

She wanted to bite him.

Not the passing thought of a violent act of defiance, but a powerful urge. She wanted to feel the texture of flesh between her teeth and revel in the pulsing heat of his blood. Nothing else would have taken the edge off. Mark's pain and shock would have just been a bonus.

Her stomach surprised her with a loud rumble. The sensation was so unusual Cecelia stopped and clasped her hands over her belly. She'd starved herself for so long that the emptiness was comfortable. The buried ache of hunger rising in her midsection was an alien sensation. Almost like tiny teeth in the lining of her gut gnawing inside her.

Stress. It had to be stress.

She pressed on. Each step broke the flawless surface of fresh snow until she came to a dotted line of shadowed tracks. The bisected impression of cloven hooves stamped in the snow were as big around as her open hand. A moose? New Hampshire was the land of moose and bears.

The tracks swept in a long arc toward the lodge, so she decide to follow them. The shadows of the pines stretched long and dark over the powdered hills, and though she was in no hurry to be back in the presence of Mark or Katherine, freezing in the dark was not a good alternative.

The crunch of snow beneath her feet fell into a rhythm as she traced the tracks and replaced the cloven footprints with the tread of her boots. The tracks seemed odd to her, too close together. She had never followed moose tracks in the snow before, but she imagined such a large animal wouldn't leave a pattern of footprints so similar to her own.

The warm glow of the lodge peeked through the timbers as the coming night cast the woods in a smooth blue. She stood at the end of her trail of moose tracks and her pulse quickened.

The rows of bedroom windows were dark and glossy. One of them was her own. A tingle like the touch of cold fingers brushed the back of her neck. The deep breath of a huge animal rasped behind her. Each of its breaths pushed the scent of carrion through her hair.

She couldn't move, couldn't scream. She stared at the silent rows of indifferent windows and they stared back. Her body of skin and bones would barely be a snack. There'd be no remains. It would clean its plate of her.

The gnawing hunger in her gut turned to knives. She turned in place toward the waiting dark.

Empty. Silence. Nothing but a single trail of cloven footprints stood behind her.

Cecelia woke from a deep sleep. The light of the fat, waxing moon bounced off the snow and cast her room in a silvery-blue ethereal glow. A trail of impressions in the blue-white snow cut a path all the way to her window. Her breath puffed around her face, but she didn't shiver. The pungent scent of old meat and animal musk filled her nose and mouth.

She wasn't alone. The unseen presence prickled at the back of her neck like icicle points, and her stomach knotted with fear, or hunger pains that no amount of resort steak or zinc treatments could fill. She hurt like she'd swallowed knives and curled herself around her core under the chilled blankets.

She was losing her mind. According to the professionals, she'd lost it years ago.

The deep-chested rush of animal breathing rasped at her back again. She squeezed her eyes shut. Tears stung like ice. The breathing continued, in concert with the pounding of her heart.

It wanted her. Whatever it was, demon, spirit, monster. It wanted her the moment she set foot on the mountain. The cutting pain in the pit of her stomach bound them.

She rolled over to face it.

A towering shape, gaunt as a shadow, stood in her bedroom. Its cloven hooves shimmered with frost, and patchy clumps of ashen fur dangled from the sharp angles of its emaciated body. Glistening black talons hooked its thick twin fingers and thumb, and bone white antlers crowned its head and nearly scraped the ceiling. Two points of pale fire burned in the hollow sockets of its skeletal, deerlike face. Its open maw was full of fangs.

A nightmare. That creature could have never made it into her room with no noise. Cecelia shut her eyes and prayed for consciousness, but the groan of her mattress as the creature pressed its misshapen hands down to lean over her body brought her back to the present. She willed her eyes to open. The arctic chill of its carrion breath rushed over her face and froze her tears to her cheeks.

The numb calm of impending death stiffened her limbs. In the beast's eyes she saw the vast cruelty of winter and abandonment. It was the endless night which no fire could warm. The hunger no flesh could fill. It was missing something so vital it would never be full.

It was missing her.

Cecelia pushed the bedroom door open. She stared for a long time, fixated on the slight rise and fall of the twin lumps draped beneath the blanket.

Katherine stirred. “Cecelia? Go back to bed.”

Mark rolled over with a groan, then propped himself up. “Can’t we get one goddamned night of peace? You can apologize in the morning, go.”

“I’m hungry.”

A shred of maternity softened the expression on Katherine’s face, such a rare, thin thing. She sat up and pulled the covers back before Mark caught her arm.

“She knows where the kitchenette is,” he said. “Cecelia, take responsibility for yourself. You’re not a child.”

She watched that spot on Mark’s chin. That stubborn, enticing spot. Saliva coated her tongue and filled the channels between her cheeks and teeth.

“Mark!” Katherine yanked her arm out of his grip. “If she’s hungry I’m going to feed her.”

Anger crowded the lines on Mark’s face. His breath puffed in the deepening chill. “She—”

Cecelia shut the door.

Frost sheathed the doorknob under her touch. Soon dawn would bleach the sky to the east. Soon she would lose her pain, and her name. Shrug off the last tatters of her humanity.

Still so hungry.

Her stomach gnashed on the last of its chilled, wet contents. The thin slash of dim light from the hall slid across the soft blue bedspread as she opened the door. A little bundle of warmth bulged in the center of the bed. Warm. So warm. Soft.

Her steps fell in silence as she crept into the room like mist. Moonlight kissed the young boy's round cheeks and dark hair. Drool slicked her chin. Her teeth throbbed. The sweet scent of breath and life freshened the faint scent of waste and decay from the hall. Voracious need raked her guts but her eyes watered. Icy tracks flowed down her blood-stained face.

The boy shifted. A tiny sigh fell from his lips with a puff of steam. Lashes fluttered.

"Cece?" Matty yawned.

The hunger spared nothing, but the name belonged to her just enough to lock her joints.

Matty rubbed his palms against his eyes. "Cece? Is that you?"

She backed into the hall as silently as she had entered and shut the door behind her. Cold and hunger wracked her body as she picked her way over the dark lumps of flesh and shimmering streaks of blood in the hall. The reek of death wafted from the master bedroom. Carpet squished under her steps. She took the blood splattered purse from the nightstand and continued to the bathroom.

She gutted the designer leather. Tubes and pallets of cosmetics, bottles of pills, and hair clips clattered into the sink before she found the keys to the SUV. For the first time in her life the face in the mirror didn't look fat or ugly. The rust red of dried blood caked her sharp cheeks and streaked her tangled hair. Dark shadows framed the recesses of her eyes, but there was a flicker of light in them. She leaned closer. Her breath didn't cloud the glass.

Tiny snowflakes fell in the blue of her eyes.

The glass was cool under her fingertips as she traced the contours of her cheeks and jaw with a smile.

She was beautiful. Strong. A waif no one would fuck with.

She rinsed the aftertaste of Mark out of her mouth, scrubbed the blood from her cheeks, and twisted her hair back with one of Katherine's clips. After a moment, she stripped out of her saturated nightshirt and left it on the bathroom floor, then traced the ridges of her ribs. She pulled on a pair of jeans then took her ski jacket from her bedroom and zipped it to her throat and returned to the soft, warm boy in the smallest bedroom.

Matty sat up in bed, scrubbed his tiny fist against the dark well of one eye.

"Cece? Why are you awake?"

She could never leave him alone.

Cecelia closed the distance to his bedside in five long strides and scooped him up. He seemed feather-light, like her.

"Close your eyes? Okay?"

"Where are we going?"

She ruffled her sticky fingers in his hair and held his head to her shoulder. His chubby cheek burned against the curve of her neck. She padded into the hall and headed toward the front door.

"We're going sledding."

BIOLOGICAL IMPERATIVE

By
Jennifer Loring

Denial, she supposed, had always been a fundamental part of human nature. It was why Bing Crosby crooned "Rudolph the Red-Nosed Reindeer" from the PA system, why the nurses had set up the ancient plastic Christmas tree across from their station and dressed the doorways with garland. Sometimes the only way you could get through another day was to pretend.

Dr. Banner Thomas—her parents couldn't have given her a more pretentious name if they'd taken high tea with the King of England while Mom was in labor—peeled off the government-mandated surgical mask worn in virtually all public areas. The government didn't mandate it there because, well, it was a hospital. The staff could hold their own against infection. Funny, the resources that people believed they had despite a finite number of beds and even fewer vaccine doses.

The lights flickered and fizzed with the threat of another brownout. Half the world warred over the last few drops of oil, and several countries held the dubious distinction of being Earth's first nuclear wastelands. No one wanted to state the obvious, but sooner than anyone cared to admit—and in a country woefully unprepared for the eventuality—after one more blackout, the power might never come back on again.

So, America kept up appearances, just like everyone else who could afford it. *For the kids*, they told themselves, in some unspoken collective guilt over having brought children into this world in the first place. Every now and then, knowing the writing had been on the wall and then some when her parents conceived her thirty-five years ago, Banner resented being there, too.

"Dr. Thomas." The unit's head nurse, Jay, waved a chart at her. No chance even to grab a cup of the asphalt the hospital called coffee, and the last coffee shop in the neighborhood had closed five months ago. Banner snatched the file and walked down the corridor toward her office. Jay tagged along behind her.

"Just five minutes, Jay." She flapped the manila folder to dismiss her. "That's all I ask."

"You don't understand."

She unlocked her office door, tossed the file onto her desk, and clicked on the TV. She spent so much time there she didn't even have a TV or cable at home. Nothing was on anymore except news, one tragedy or another from around the world. African countries depopulated by AIDS. China threatening to nuke India over water resources. Another island nation drowned by rising sea levels.

"The patient was brought in a few hours ago. She has a hundred-and-four-degree fever, complains of severe fatigue, muscle stiffness, coughing—"

"Sounds like the flu."

Jay's face was a color wheel of emotions. His fingers clenched and unclenched at his sides. She knew he wouldn't let himself fly off the handle; he needed the job too badly. Hell, they all did, but she'd never seen him react like that before. He had been there for so long, experienced so much, that nothing seemed to faze him anymore. But he was trembling, and his eyes pleaded with her in some implicit terror whose source she had already begun to suspect. It had been all over the news for weeks.

"She started . . . bleeding."

"Okay," Banner said at last. "I'll take a look at her right now."

Over the speakers, Peggy Lee sang that she had seen Mommy kissing Santa Claus. Banner followed Jay down to ICU, where he handed her another surgical mask. She slipped it on and opened the door.

In the bed lay a woman—a girl, really, seventeen, maybe eighteen—connected to an IV unit and oxygen tubes. The heart-rate monitor beeped steadily but much more slowly than it should have. Rust-colored stains darkened her cheeks, her lips and chin, the sides of her neck. No family or loved ones lingered outside, waiting for the doctor to reassure them she would make a full recovery.

As if reading her mind, Jay said, "She's from the slums. I don't think she has any family. She appears to be a prostitute and intravenous drug user."

"They don't have much else left down there," Banner muttered. She pressed her stethoscope against the girl's chest. Her heart thumped once every couple of seconds, but with a fever like hers, Banner would've expected it to be racing. Her breath, too, came as shallow, barely perceptible rises of her breast. Banner turned over her arm.

The rash always manifested in the softest areas first; the inner arm or thigh, the stomach, the buttocks. Because it looked like a harmless fungal infection, tinea versicolor or at worst ringworm, quarantines and checkpoints hadn't halted its spread. They couldn't tell everyone with a minor rash to stay home, but by the time major symptoms emerged, it had spread to everyone they knew.

Or flown halfway across the world to a new country. And in the slums, of course, the ones already sick, on drugs, eating once a day if that and even then out of dumpsters, were the canaries in the coal mine. You knew it was too late only when blood began to leak from the nose, mouth, and eyes. Something like Ebola, which in its natural state killed far too quickly to be an effective weapon, that had been weaponized to be as contagious as a common cold. Someone had done his or her homework.

"Quarantine her," Banner said. "You know there's nothing else we can do for her."

Jay, his mouth set into a grim line, called for a couple of orderlies to transport the girl a short distance down the hall and advised the unit to avoid her passage. Banner retreated to her office. She could do little for any of them, infected or not. Just one of her many failures.

Like most young doctors, she'd had nothing but the noblest of intentions. She would treat the people in the slums, stop the spread of at least a few diseases. Save lives no one else thought worth the trouble. The world had other plans.

The soldier at the checkpoint, recognizing Banner's hospital badge, waved her over the bridge. Some governmental entity—city, state, who knew—used to hang a giant glowing snowflake on either side just after Thanksgiving every year. Now they were lucky the rusting, flaking overpass hadn't already crashed into the river. Just a matter of time. Infrastructure all over the country was deteriorating at a rate no miraculous infusion of cash could have prevented. And there wasn't any cash anyway.

Like anyone with a few dollars to scrape together, she had fled uptown after the first flood left a city filled with rotting garbage and dead fish from the river. The viral outbreaks began in earnest then, and it wasn't unusual for her to pull thirty-six-hour shifts. It assuaged her guilt for having abandoned her patients to the ravaged slums, where even consistent electricity had become a luxury. It was all coming apart at the seams, and everyone knew it. The problem was that no one wanted to talk about it. Acknowledgement made it real, and no one knew what to do.

The Interstate wound around blocks of apartments spray-painted with gang tags, where prostitutes and drug dealers plied their trades even in broad daylight, since the city had laid off most public servants months ago. They didn't exactly have other options. Walmart remained, the proverbial cockroach, but the once-vibrant downtown core was an ocean of abandoned storefronts, theaters, and restaurants haunted by the dead dreams of so many who had come here to make a better life. Many of them lurked in the guttering streetlights, skin pockmarked with needle tracks and meth sores, eyes devoid of all hope.

A woman lunged at someone—her lover, her pimp, her dealer—with flailing arms, jaws snapping like a feral dog's. Banner shook her head and returned her focus to the mostly empty, rain-slicked asphalt. Increasingly violent behavior seemed an inevitable side effect of drugs these days. The bath-salt zombies from a couple of decades ago had been just the tip of the iceberg. Week after week, victims passed through the ER with tongues torn out, eyes gouged, ears, lips, or noses ripped off. Fingers and entire limbs all but rent from bodies.

Ten minutes later, Banner pulled the used Chevy Cavalier into her garage. The door lowered immediately behind her. She unlocked the side door to the kitchen, then dead-bolted and chained it. The front door remained dead-bolted at all times, the windows barred and locked. Sure, she was paranoid. She may not have been able to articulate the vague, niggling fear chewing at the back of her brain, but the tipping point would arrive sooner rather than later.

An instrumental version of "Jingle Bells" tinkled cheerfully from the PA system, and empty cardboard boxes wrapped like presents gleamed beneath the fake tree. Jay met her at the doors, his face as pale as the snow that had begun to fall and his expression incongruous with the otherwise happy scene. He wore a full biohazard suit with mask. It was going to be that kind of day.

"She's gone."

"Like I said, there was nothing we could do for her. There's no known treatment yet—"

"No. She's *gone*. I mean, yes, she died. I *saw* her die. We left the room for no more than five minutes, and when we came back, she was gone."

After Banner put on a suit of her own, Jay all but dragged her to the quarantine area, just beyond ICU. The door flap on the bright orange tent had not been opened as much as shredded. Tubes and needles lay on the bed or the floor, damp with blood and mucus. With nothing to monitor, the machines waited quietly for a directive.

Banner's stomach dropped. If not for being one of the only hospitals still in operation, they could have kissed their jobs goodbye with the biggest lawsuit in state history. The real problem was that their walking biohazard compromised the health and safety of every single person in the building. Any one of them, or all of them, might be infected now.

"And no one saw an allegedly dead woman get up, pull out all her tubes, and walk away? None of the nurses or orderlies? The security guard? No one?"

"I don't know what's going on, Banner. It's been crazy here, but I notified the entire floor that we had a quarantine situation. Everyone knew."

His hands were shaking. His fingertips were still yellow, though he'd told Banner he had tried to quit smoking when the damned things shot up to twenty-five bucks a pack. He looked like he could use a couple now. Banner, for her part, wished for a Scotch on the rocks. Or several.

"You're sure she was dead."

"Jesus Christ, Banner. I've been a nurse for twenty years."

"Sorry. I just … We need to get this place on lockdown. If no one's seen her, she must still be here somewhere. Go upstairs and tell Dr. Sellars what happened."

The chief of staff had very few meetings to attend these days, but it wasn't the fear of interrupting that made Jay hesitate. Finally, he headed for the decontamination area. Banner lingered a bit longer, examining the tent as if it were a crime scene, yet nothing pointed her in the right direction. Blood crusted the sheet and pillow, old blood, but not the floor.

The lights fizzed and flickered. And this time they went out.

"What do you mean, we can't leave?" a woman screamed over the unit clerk's desk. "It's almost Christmas!"

Jay held his hand over the mouthpiece of the phone receiver. The emergency generator had kicked on, leaving the hospital in the dimmest of lighting so that it could divert power to the most critical facilities. Heat was unfortunately another one of the major casualties, and only the faint suggestion of such wafted from the vents. "Ma'am, please give me just one moment."

"I want answers *now*!"

Banner grasped the woman's arm and pulled her aside. "Ma'am, we are very sorry for the inconvenience, but the city is requiring everyone to stay here until we can determine who is and isn't infected. It's not up to us."

"That could take days!"

"I understand, ma'am, and we're doing everything we can to get you out of here before Christmas."

"How did this happen? When do we get answers?"

"As soon as the health department has finished its investigation, we'll share what we know."

The woman sighed, rolled her eyes, and jerked her arm away. She flung herself into a chair like a sullen teenager. So much for good will to men and the rest of those meaningless holiday platitudes.

Jay set the phone down. The watery light deepened the lines in his face, lines Banner hadn't noticed earlier that day. To be fair, she'd certainly sprung a few new gray hairs. She wished she could send him home, give him the vacation and the time with his family that he deserved. His husband had lost his job a few months ago, and if either of them was being honest, his prospects of landing another were slim to none.

"I need a cigarette," he muttered. "Thanks for dealing with her."

"My pleasure. Okay, that's a lie."

Jay laughed and ran both hands through his hair. "Someone really screwed up, Banner. And if we tell these people it's red fever, there's going to be a riot."

"I know. Let me see if security's had any luck finding her. I'll be back soon."

Banner stopped at the utility closet and dug out a flashlight. She made her way to the security desk in the now-frigid foyer, where the guard shivered and stared at the locked automatic doors. Snow clung to the sidewalk, the cars. Only wan moonlight muted by the clouds lit the crystalline world.

"Hear from anybody yet?"

The guard leapt a couple inches from his stool, then exhaled loudly and chuckled. "You scared the crap out of me, Dr. Thomas. No, haven't heard anything. Of course, all the cameras are down, so… But I can tell you for sure she hasn't tried getting out this way."

"Thanks. Can you radio up there and let them know I'm coming up anyway? Seems like we should've had an update by now."

"Sure thing." The guard unclipped his walkie-talkie and held it up to his mouth. "Security, this is front desk. Do you copy?"

A sizzle of static. The guard frowned and shook the radio. "Just changed the batteries this morning."

"Don't worry about it. I'll find out what's going on." Banner clapped the guard on the shoulder and passed back through the ER, bypassing the nonfunctional elevators for the staircase. She pushed open the metal door and took the stairs two at a time. Now that the PA was dead, an eerie silence descended over the hospital, so that she could almost hear the whisper of snow against the outer walls.

The bar on the door clanged as she pressed it open, a sound in the stillness like a blacksmith's hammer on iron. Because it contained only offices, the third floor was even quieter and darker than the rest of the building. Banner pointed the flashlight beam at the carpet before her and took a few steps forward, suppressing the urge to run for it like a child diving onto her bed, afraid of the monsters underneath.

Why does the damned office have to be all the way at the end of the hall?

The shadows emitted a low, throaty growl. A closet by the office housed some kind of mechanical apparatus, maybe another vital system failing, but she was no engineer. She could radio maintenance from the security office and have them take a look. Banner opened the office door to utter blackness, a bank of dead monitors for the blinded cameras. The rumble came again, not human but not machinery, either. Her flashlight beam caught a gleam of dark liquid splashed on the console. She raised the light; more dark liquid spattered the monitors, the walls, even the ceiling.

Banner illuminated the chairs where the two officers, or what was left of them, maintained the hospital's safety. Much like the ICU patients Banner had seen over recent months, they'd suffered attacks so violent she was at a loss to explain their cause. She tried to put out of her mind the rumors she'd heard about red fever, impossible rumors fed by people with no medical knowledge. Even the most basic biology education—and she wasn't certain the charter schools the state had mandated to replace all the public schools still taught it—would erase any notions of its plausibility.

But biology, or at least biology as she understood it, ceased to matter in that instant. Because despite Jay's confirmation of the girl's death, she crouched there in the doorway and snarled at Banner.

"Stay there, sweetheart," Banner cooed, hands outstretched in a gesture of surrender. "We're all here to help you. You're very sick, and we've got to get you back to your room, okay?" She glanced back at the security office. She should have grabbed one of the radios so she could call for orderlies—

The girl knocked Banner to the ground before her next breath, and Banner raised her arm to keep snapping jaws from tearing into her face. Long strings of saliva dribbled onto her chin and neck. The girl's breath stank of blood and raw meat, a butcher shop. The image of the woman in the slums assaulting her companion flashed through Banner's mind. As with all the other problems they faced, she'd have to acknowledge just how badly they'd all screwed up. The red fever had been there for months, in some new and terrible form.

"Someone help me!" she shouted. Doors clicked and swung open, but the girl had already sunk her teeth into Banner's forearm. In the violet-hot agony that followed, she could almost feel the virus leaping from mouth to wound, a million microscopic assassins usurping control of her body.

"Somebody do something!"

Dr. Sellars peered out from his office, his face so white it nearly glowed. "My God," he murmured. Someone broke the emergency firebox and charged at the girl with a hand axe, though the darkness and pain blinded Banner to her would-be savior. The girl's skull split like an overripe fruit, splashing blood and brain onto Banner's coat, her face. Not that it mattered. The girl had already performed her biological imperative.

She had reproduced.

The room was cold, and metal gleamed beneath fluorescent lights. An overturned cart of tweezers, forceps, scissors, and scalpels littered the white tile floor. She rested upon a table with only a paper sheet to cover her. Half-remembered words flitted through her churning brain. *Surgery? Hospital?* They couldn't leave someone to sleep here. This wasn't a proper room, not even a proper bed, and besides, she could not recall having gotten sick.

Splashes of blood stained the steel door across from her. A body wearing a once-white coat lay on the floor in a crimson pool, one arm outstretched toward the door handle. The ragged wounds on its legs, stripped to the bone from ankle to pubis, suggested an animal attack. She slid off the table and fell to her hands and knees, forgetting for a moment how to walk. A vague sense of having forgotten many things plagued her. Worse was the idea that she should not be there at all. Her legs finally obeyed with a stiff and peculiar kinesis, as though she had not used her limbs in some time. She pulled the door open and looked back at the body, which stirred in her a sense of great urgency.

The feculent hall outside was a claustrophobic space with low ceilings and walls that seemed to close in. The dining hall lay to her left. Beneath the stench of putrefying flesh, she detected rotten food. Under that, antiseptics and formaldehyde.

People lay draped over tables and chairs, people on the floor, people divested of tissue like the man in the other room. A glaze blurred her vision, and so she understood the dark smears on the walls and floors to be blood mostly by its scent. Other humanoid shapes shambled amongst the corpses. They too stank of decay. Some hunched beside the bodies and scooped out the last remnants of innards, or gnawed upon what few limbs had not been entirely defleshed.

She touched one of her eyes, which felt gelatinous and gooey. She pushed open a door with a vaguely familiar black-and-white symbol on it and found a grotesque figure in the mirror. Something about the image reflected back at her compelled her to prod it with one finger; the doppelgänger mocked her every movement, poking at the cold, hard glass from the other side. The lips pulled away from blackened and receding gums, making the teeth appear much longer. Hair protruded from the tight scalp in pale brown wisps.

Deep in the recesses of her brain, where a handful of neurons still fired, she understood the reflection as her own image. Her skin itched and came off in flakes beneath her cracked, yellow nails. Stitches ran from her groin all the way up to her chest, as if someone had sawed her in two. She half-remembered seeing people like that before, more wreckage from the nightmare that besieged her.

The odor of putrefaction followed her like a ghost. Another fragment of memory awakened amongst neurons not reduced to basic electrical impulses and primal needs, but not enough to understand more than that she was very hungry.

She passed a newspaper kiosk on her way back down the hall. How quickly those ciphers, of which some troubling part of her insisted she ought to know, slipped away from her grasp. And the harder she tried to hold onto them, the quicker they disappeared.

words...?

w...

...

Still, the bold black headline suggested something terribly important. Of the most importance to *her*, however, was the impatient hunger that forced her to keep searching for the elusive thing she could not vocalize or even fully comprehend. She found a staircase and, clutching the railing, slowly ascended. An odd sound stopped her for a moment until she realized it was her own moaning voice. The almost painful hunger seeped into her flesh and bones to remind her with each ferocious creak and pop of her joints that she was falling apart.

On the second floor, she heard the pathetic mewl of a sick animal. She began to salivate, so much that it dribbled down her chin in long, mucousy strands. She followed the sound and the smell of human excrement that accompanied it past a bank of windows with the curtains drawn. The source of the noise, though muted behind glass. The place that guarded the live thing she sought.

She opened the door onto rows of tiny beds, and in them dozens of squalling infants. Many more were clearly dead, their flesh—if they still had flesh—gray and their lips blue. Those still crying resembled shrieking lumps of decayed meat. They looked like her. As she shuffled between beds they snapped their toothless jaws at her, but she ignored them.

At the back of the room, she lifted a thin, pale baby from its bed. The child, spared whatever had befallen the others, would not live much longer. These creatures needed food as all living things did. As *she* did.

She remembered something, that these creatures came from women; to a woman this one would return. She sank her nails into its flesh, and it screamed; it curled its hands into tiny fists as though it would attack her. Its skin smelled of powder and sour milk, its diaper of shit. She opened her mouth and slammed her teeth down on the baby's left side like a bear trap. The child stopped writhing and fell silent.

Raw and untainted, the meat would quell her appetite. The meat would stop famine from tearing apart her bones.

She needed more.

She sensed more nearby. It possessed a different aroma—the tang of past illnesses, of sex, of sweat glands—than that in the nursery. An adult. She walked down the hall to an office with closed blinds and a locked door. Her heightened sense of smell assured her of meat inside. She threw herself against the door until the wood splintered and broke and she could reach in to unlock it.

A man cowered beneath a metal desk. He looked up and screamed, as taken aback by the sight as his intruder had been upon looking in the mirror. Quivering, he held up his hands, and she thought—or what passed for thought to her remaining brain cells—she ought to know who he was, that he had once been someone important to her. His eyes reflected terror and something the woman recalled from another life, if indeed she had ever lived another life. Madness.

“Banner…? Oh, God… They have soldiers surrounding the city. They’re talking about tactical nukes. They left us here to die—on Christmas!” White puffs escaped his mouth with each word, though she did not understand what the man said. There was only hunger, elemental and omnipotent.

In order to ease the agony that tunneled deep into her marrow, the flesh must be alive. She fell on the man like a starving wolf, shredding flesh with her teeth and nails, gorging herself on all the juicy, salty delicacies of the human body. Her mouth more canine than human now as she crushed the man’s skull. She could smell it, the spongy pink organ protected by this thick layer of bone. The source of life.

As she departed the office, she scraped her arms on the doorway and left shreds of skin behind. Her muscles already cried out for more sustenance, and a low, plaintive moan escaped her desiccated lips. She pushed open a door and stood in a lot strewn with metallic lumps coated in a colorless substance, which stirred further ambiguous memories.

Unable to block out the bright sunlight or form tears, her eyes simply dried out. All the colors of the world evaporated into shades of gray, its structures and creatures reduced to ambiguous shadows. Sight had fled from her at last, but she did not need it. The air dripped with the perfume of humanity’s flesh.

She had awakened from a dream of decades. She dreamed she was once a woman in a white coat; she dreamed she was once a baby writhing in a tiny bed. But these amorphous images, and all that might have been the last splinters of memory, drowned in the rising tide of everlasting hunger.

MOON TIME

by
Christe M. Callabro

I look at my reflection in the mirror, like I do every morning, and overanalyze myself, trying to find any differences. Positive ones, anyway. Today my lips are too chapped, my face too red, my hair too scraggly. I examine every pore of the skin I can see, suck my stomach in and out, look for new divots in my butt. All the same as yesterday. Yay. I haven't changed. But still, something feels different, low and primal in my gut.

It's coming, and it's too soon. God, I haven't even gotten over the last time. I still feel so tired, so up and down. Women always complain about their periods being from hell but mine seems determined to drag me back to its home. Every month it arrives with a little more violence, and takes more of my energy when it leaves. I even swore last time that I may have blacked out for a minute, once or twice. Or maybe my memory is just going. Who knows. It just feels like there are tiny tears in my memory, and no amount of gingko biloba or celery juice or whatever the hell they're recommending this hour can fix it.

I look in the mirror and force myself to smile. All the bullshit positive affirmations you're supposed to tell your reflection just wither in my throat. I cannot feel anything at the moment except disgust and dread, yet still I keep smiling until my teeth ache. My reflection smiles back, a joker's grin, and I swear there is poison in her eyes, a sinister glee when her teeth flash. I blink slowly.

Nope. I look normal.

What the hell is wrong with me?

"God, Diane, you are such a bitch today. Are you on your period again? Or is it just the full moon is coming up and everyone is going to be an asshole today." Sil laughed and winked at me, expecting me to crack open, reveal the soft center that is usually on display for the world to see, laughing at my own expense. I oblige her, but she is too focused on her phone and her fifty-seven followers and her ego to see that I am only laughing on the outside, that my eyes are really seeing her head smashed against the wall, neck angled too sharply, blood and soft things mingling with the stains from someone's splattered lunch.

I blink, and Sil is staring at me, her smile nervous and fading fast from her lips. I realize I am still laughing. I shake my head to get the image to dissipate.

"Yeah, it's hitting me pretty hard this time too. I feel like I just had it. I haven't even recovered from the last one." It is very hard to focus on her plain, intact face when I swore just a moment ago it was crunched up on the wall.

Jesus, what is wrong with me?

I've had plenty of macabre fantasies before, out of anger, or desperation, or hormones, but this . . . Normal me, even dark depressed emo normal me, would never actually entertain or even envision something as … primal as that. That blood-soaked and violent. But Sil is right about one thing—it is that time of the month, or it will be in a day or so. And with each cycle comes more and more blood, and more pain. More helplessness and rage and longing for the freedom to just do what I want …

"Girl, don't take this the wrong way, but you seem like you *always* have your period. You probably need to see a doctor." She shifts and gets up from her seat at the break room table. "Seriously. You leave that unchecked long enough and it'll really mess with your life."

I fight to keep the sneer from reaching my lips.

Girl, you have no idea.

When I get home from work, Trevor is just pulling up to the house. His consistent presence is still fairly new in my life, but for the most part I'm still enjoying the shininess of a new relationship and all the fun physicalities that go with it. I know he is eager to see me but I'm afraid he's going to be disappointed when he finds out about my early visitor. He's just one of those guys that doesn't want to get messy. Doesn't matter that my libido is through the roof at that point. Or that we can still do stuff that doesn't involve mess, though if I'm being honest, the feeling of being speared through while my insides are already in turmoil just sends me over the edge. Maybe a good fucking will loosen everything up and my body will stop feeling so expectant and full.

I tell him. He looks equal parts annoyed and strangely hungry.

"You're getting it again so soon? That doesn't seem right. Maybe you really should see a doctor."

"Yeah, a girl I work with said the same thing."

He steps close and hugs me, offering a comfort that fails to really understand. I can't appreciate it, even though I want to.

He leans down and murmurs against my ear.

"Well, I guess we should get things moving then, before you get too gunky, right?"

I loathe the way he says it, even though my body automatically responds, hands on autopilot undoing my jeans, hips already primed and open. His touch is rushed, like he instinctively wants to be in and out before the floodgates release. I refuse to ever tell him how horny I actually get during my period. He wouldn't get it. Or worse, he'd try to get it, for my sake, but I would always know deep down inside he'd be disgusted by the blood.

I want to just enjoy myself before my body betrays me. Maybe I should find someone who truly doesn't care, that I can use and ride whenever I want, that would welcome the sight of my thighs stained with blood . . .

I blink, and Trevor is under me, hand on my breast, his face confused. "You . . . never moved like that before. Are you okay?"

I want to say *I'm sorry, I don't know what's come over me*. What comes out of my mouth instead is, "Didn't you like it?"

He grins slowly, a dark glint in his eye. “I fucking love it. You should take charge more often.”

I look down at his sweat-slicked chest, my nails dug into his flesh for grip. Is that what I’m doing? Taking charge?

That’s not very like me.

After a few hours with Trevor I beg for some solitude. Thankfully I can use the period card to say I’m not feeling well and just need to rest. I know he wants to take care of me, but tonight I need to be alone with my body and the fullness and my feelings, see if I can make any sense of what is happening to me. Why I feel different.

I stare out at the full moon hanging huge and pregnant over my neighbor’s house. It’s one of those low super moons that apparently mean all sorts of extra magic bullshit for your horoscope. I think this one even has some ridiculous and too-appropriate name like the Super Blood Wolf Moon. My hippy friend that works at the health food store always talks about the moon’s pull on her life, how its energy makes her career more engaging even though she’s just an assistant manager, how it bodes well for her love life even though her boyfriend cheated on her but she still won’t leave him. She even calls her period her “moon time.” Like the moon really has anything to do with it.

Or maybe it does. Maybe this too-full feeling, this stabbing knife that’s sitting low in my guts, maybe that’s the moon’s fault. It reminds me of those horror movies where someone’s possessed, or pregnant with a demon baby, and the person’s stomach is just moving around, skin molding into grotesque shapes pushing up from the muscles. Maybe if I lift my shirt and look at my stomach, I’ll see what’s filling me up and pushing from the inside out.

It makes sense to me. Why else would I have my period so often? There has got to be something in there, something feeding on that one kind of blood, something making me lose little snippets of myself. What other explanation could there be?

I blink. The moon doesn't. It just looks through me.

Maybe a bath would make me feel better.

Usually I count myself fortunate that I have a window in my bathroom, but the way the full moon is just hanging there staring at me like a creeper while I undress unnerves me tonight. I'm not myself anyway, my body is so tired each movement is like dragging my limbs through syrup. Or blood. Is blood really that thick? Well, menstrual blood certainly seems so.

I turn off the water and check the temperature. Just short of boiling my flesh off my bones, which is how I like it. Normally I put Epsom salts or a bath bomb or something in the water, something to change the environment, make me feel pretty and pampered and like I'm in a spa commercial and not my shabby bathroom with the moon judging me through the sheers. No, tonight, if there's blood in the water, I want to see it. At least then I'll have confirmation that it's back.

I slide my undies off right before hopping into the still slightly too-hot water. There's a couple of rusty stains on my preemptive pad, but no telltale spots of bright red or dark goo. That means tomorrow will be the bad day, when it all comes gushing out and I have to make all the excuses for why my body likes to go crazy when I bleed. The water instantly puckers my feet and fingers, and my skin feels cold and burny at the same time. Probably too hot still, but I don't care. Maybe it'll finish what Trevor started and knock something inside me loose, or burn it out of my body. Sterilize me, clean me off, clean me out. I lean back against my bath pillow and close my eyes.

Maybe I'll drown.

I open my eyes and blink.

Why would I want to drown? Is that even my voice inside my head?

My guts rumble and shift. The cramps are stupid terrible this time around. Sometimes sex makes them feel better but not today. I close my eyes again. I just want to enjoy my bath for a few minutes without pain, without feeling like I need to get out of the tub and use the toilet, without hearing anything in my head but the bathroom fan running and the distant highway traffic outside.

I must have fallen asleep. My eyes reluctantly open, eyelids sticky and crusted. It takes me a minute to realize my bathwater is red.

Not just red, but thick, opaque. When I move my legs it slides over my skin like oil.

What the hell?

I know I wanted to see blood in the water, but this . . . ?

I am completely covered in blood.

The tub is full of blood and even has some floating clots for good measure, dark little islands in this literal red tide that I am sitting in, and the bath is still too hot, and my skin is puckering and burning all over. I look up at the window and the moon is right there, a spotlight in my eyes, peeping at the mess I'm in. Is this blood all mine? Is this what I was filled with?

On the surface of the blood, between the clots and the twin points of my knees, the reflection of the moon shines full and round. Or maybe that's my overhead light. Oh, no, it's moving up and out of the water/blood, taking a shape, not a reflection of the moon at all. The circle rises up, becomes the top of a head, a face dripping in gore, hair streaming like burgundy ribbons around her shoulders. A torso next, then two arms that loosely reach toward me. She looks at me and smiles, like she did this morning in the mirror, undaunted by the fact that she looks like something out of a horror movie.

That sweet poison is still in her eyes.

She is my reflection after all.

I lean forward, detached from fear, to take a closer look at her, this other me I just gave birth to in a water bath like they do at the natural birth center. Except the water is supposed to wash away the birthing fluid. She leans forward too, curious. Her expression must mirror what's on my face, since she is me, right? I am seeing the moon me, the blood me, the one everyone else seems to see when it's that time of the month.

But in the end, she is still me.

Isn't she?

She reaches forward and cups my face with her slick hot hands. Sticky sludge drips from her elbows back into the tub. I too reach forward, mirroring her, and press my palms to her drying red cheeks. It's only fair—if she is my reflection, then I should be hers too. Doesn't she deserve that? Does a reflection deserve anything?

"Yes," she says. "Yes I do."

Her hands grip the sides of my face, thumbs sliding over my cheekbones.

"I deserve freedom."

Before I can mirror her, she is pushing me down, down, under the water, which is actually the thickest blood possible. I gasp and the blood sucks up into my nose, pours through my surprised open mouth down my throat, coating everything, gunking me all up, going back to the place it came from.

My tub is so deep. Where is the surface? Are her hands even still pushing me down, or am I stuck too fast, my mouth too full of iron and clot to even scream for help?

Do I need help?

Do I?

I look at myself in the mirror, like I do every morning, and begin to analyze myself. Then I stop. Who the hell cares what this shell looks like? It looks like freedom to me.

I smile at my reflection, and it smiles back at me, but it almost looks forced, the eyes just a little sad.

I blink, and look again.

Nope. I look normal.

And I feel great.

THUS DO WE REACH TO THE STARS

by
Michelle R. Lane

Crushing on jackasses was my *raison d'être*. The more inappropriate a man was, the more attractive he became. Jimmy was my latest obsession. He was married, he had two kids, and he was my boss.

I should have known better, but it's hard to break bad habits. I made the mistake of thinking he wanted to take our friendship to the next level when he invited me to New Orleans for a conference. We were getting drunk in a dive bar in the French Quarter when he destroyed my fantasy of finding true happiness in his pants. I wasn't an expert at flirting, but when you put your hand on a guy's thigh and smile at him, most men get the hint you're into them. He ignored my advances and talked about how attractive he found all the other women in the bar. Was Jimmy really *that* stupid?

I drained my Manhattan and stood up with my purse in hand. "You make me feel like I'm at a high school dance, covered in weeping sores," I said.

Jimmy grabbed my arm a little too tightly. "I said I'm sorry."

"Sorry? I haven't felt this bad since the first time my boyfriend turned out to be gay."

"You've had more than one gay boyfriend?"

I rolled my eyes and brushed away the sweaty curls plastered to my forehead. "Apparently, I'm the cure for sexual uncertainty. But that's not the point."

"What is your point?"

I shifted my weight from one foot to the other, tucked my clutch under my armpit, and rested my fist on my ample hip. His gaze followed the shape of my curves. I wanted to scream at him: *My eyes are up here, asshole!* But the truth was, I liked the attention.

"You eyeballed every other woman in this place and shouted into my ear, 'She's hot, she's hot, she's hot,' like I'm a dude."

"I'm still not following you," he said.

I popped the last cigarette from our shared pack into my mouth, sighed deeply, and lit it. My head hurt from the heat and the twenty minutes of crying I'd done in the bathroom. This conversation wasn't helping.

"Earlier this evening, you opened your soul like a festering wound for me to gaze upon and told me wildly inappropriate and intimate details about your life," I said.

"Yeah, because I thought we were friends," he said.

I shook my head. "Maybe if David Lynch is defining the word 'friends.'"

"What the fuck is that supposed to mean?"

"You showed me a picture of your wife's latest surgery. She's missing an ear. Normal people don't show things like that to each other," I said above the din of the music.

Jimmy frowned at me, clearly confused. "You're one of my closest friends."

"Right. You led me to believe that your feelings for me went beyond friendship, but now you act like my vagina is nonexistent."

He released his grip on my arm. "What?"

I gestured with my hand like a camera taking a panoramic shot of the bar. "Of all the women in this bar, I'm the only one you have the slightest chance of impressing and you aren't even remotely interested in having sex with me. I care about you, but we're done."

"Wait, you want me to fuck you?"

Before I turned to leave, I jerked my thumb at a skinny blonde near the exit and shouted over Iron Maiden. "Maybe she'll let me borrow her body since you aren't interested in mine."

The sounds of heavy metal faded behind me as I made my way across a tiny footbridge. I imagined myself as an angry Godzilla stomping through a set of miniature Jimmys in a B–horror flick. Brick dust crumbled to the pavement as I slid against the walls of the narrow alleyway and back onto Toulouse. I was headed as far away from Bourbon Street as I could get.

Fuck the drunken tourists. Fuck Jimmy, that slimy little fuckhead.

Hot tears mixed with the sweat on my cheeks. I'd made a scene at the bar and acted like a fool. As a rule, I tried to keep my emotions bottled up tight like arsenic tucked away in a glass jar high on an apothecary shelf.

I failed today.

To be fair, the true love of Jimmy's life was dying. While I understood his heartache, I also hated him for having a love of his life. She stood at the threshold to the Great Beyond and his world was coming apart. But goddamn it, how many times would I have to be the runner-up in some emotionally unavailable loser's sex life?

For now, there was a strong cocktail in the Bywater with my name on it. Probably several. If I couldn't spend my night in Jimmy's arms, I could at least get drunk and listen to a well-stocked jukebox.

I wandered into a corner bar with the Cramps blaring out of the open French doors. The music ricocheted off the punched-tin ceiling and vibrated the worn wooden floorboards. I ordered a Manhattan. My foot tapped along to the jungle pulse of "Blue Moon Baby." The first sip of my bourbon cocktail was smoky and sweet. The amber liquid slid down the back of my throat and infused my limbs with medicinal warmth. For a few moments, the music and the bourbon transported me home.

Home. Home is where the heart is. Or so they say. But I no longer had a home. Did that make me heartless as well? At thirty, I lived out of hotel rooms most of the time, traveling from place to place, trying to get my foot in the door with a major publishing house. Usually, I just found myself surrounded by drunken writers who were more successful than me.

Homeless, heartless, whatever.

All I knew was I was lonely and bored. If I wasn't careful, I'd find myself at the bottom of a bottle. It wouldn't be the first time, but it only took once to be the last.

Lonely women with self-esteem issues shouldn't drink alone in bars. Put that on a bumper sticker.

I got up to buy cigarettes from the vending machine at the back of the bar and added a few more tunes to the jukebox. I lit a Lucky Strike and punched in 3-8-0-7, Smokey Robinson & the Miracles' "Tears of a Clown."

When I returned to the bar, the seat next to mine was occupied. I couldn't see his face, but he had sandy blond hair. He was tall and slim, but built strong. A professional male armed with a tailored suit and button-down shirt.

I sat down, not looking away. He wore glasses, but no tie.

You often make passes at men who wear glasses.

I exhaled smoke from the corner of my mouth and noticed my Manhattan had a twin. I raised an eyebrow at the bartender. She winked, took the lollipop out of her mouth, and motioned towards the stranger in the seat next to mine.

Oh, what the hell? At least say something. I tapped him on the shoulder. "Um…thank you," I said.

He swiveled to face me, and I cursed the audible intake of my breath.

"I hate to drink alone. I hope you don't mind."

My cheeks burned with a blush I knew I couldn't hide. Chiseled features and hypnotic eyes. Eyes I couldn't pull away from.

It was rare for me to be at a loss for words. I had to say something.

"Vampires or werewolves?"

"Pardon?" His icy blue eyes bored into me from behind his almost invisible lenses. A smile played at the corner of his mouth.

"Which do you prefer? Vampires or werewolves?" I sipped my drink and didn't let my gaze waiver.

He ran his long, slender fingers through his businesslike haircut and reached for my pack of Luckys on the bar. He searched my face for permission and I handed him my lighter. He slid a cigarette between his lips directly from the pack and lit it with his eyes closed.

Exhaling a blue cloud through his nostrils, he set the pack back on the bar. He drained his beer and ordered another one. I handed him my Manhattan to sip while he waited. Our knees touched.

"Vampires versus werewolves, huh? Well, I suppose it depends on which legends or stories we're talking about. I mean, aside from *Dracula* and *Interview with the Vampire*, what are your favorite vampire tales?" He raised his eyebrows after the question.

I pursed my lips. "That's tough. I like so many. It might be easier to list my favorite werewolf stories."

"Fine. Let's begin with werewolves."

His beer arrived. He took a hefty pull from the Abita bottle and another drag of the cigarette.

"'The Company of Wolves' is one of my favorites."

"Ah, an Angela Carter fan. I suppose you enjoy her other naughty fairy tales, too." His smile was infectious.

I giggled and covered my laughter with my hand, almost embarrassed.

"I must admit, dark, erotic fairy tales are a lot more fun to read. Especially if they have happy endings," I said.

He was silent.

Did I go too far? Maybe I misread his cues. Flirtation does have rules. I sipped my drink and waited.

He finally spoke. "Have you read Anne Rice's Sleeping Beauty series?"

"A long time ago. I was in high school when I read them."

"Did your parents know you were reading them?"

"I was reading *Delta of Venus* and *Little Birds* by the time I turned fourteen. I kept a stash of banned books under my bed."

"Naughty and deceptive. You're a bad girl," he said.

"I thought my tattoos were a giveaway."

"It's hard to tell these days. Everyone has tattoos. It used to only be bikers, sailors, and the enlightened. Now everyone and their mother has ink."

"Do you have any tattoos?"

"Yes, but I don't show them to just anyone." He winked.

His expensive suit made me think of a birthday gift. The wrapping was nice, but I wanted what was underneath.

"Are we still talking about vampires and werewolves?" I said.

"I'm pretty sure we've moved on to fairy tales with happy endings. I'm going to go out on a limb here and guess that if you were Red Riding Hood, you'd let the Big Bad Wolf eat you."

"It's like you're right inside my head." I shivered and finished my third Manhattan.

He stood and offered me his hand. "Come. I want to show you something."

I took his hand and a kaleidoscope of butterflies took wing inside my stomach. He ordered another round of drinks and led me to a red vinyl clamshell booth. We were the only patrons seated at the back of the dimly lit bar. Neon flashed pink and green against the black and gray Formica tabletop. A waitress brought our drinks and he slipped her a twenty-dollar bill. He smiled at me and patted the seat next to him.

I couldn't help thinking, *What big teeth you have.*

"I like you," he said.

"Why?"

"You make me laugh, you're interesting to talk to, and your brown skin and curves make me wonder what you taste like." He took a sip of his beer.

I wanted to kiss him, but my deeply ingrained trust issues stopped me. "What did you want to show me?"

He unbuttoned his shirt down to his waist and I caught a glimpse of a tattoo on his chest and upper shoulder. My fingers reached out to pull the fabric open, revealing a murder of crows in the branches of a dead tree. I traced the black ink masterpiece with my fingertips. He shivered and let out a soft sigh. Our eyes met, and his gaze guided me back to the tattoo. The static image became animated as the crows flew from the tree.

Impossible.

My heartbeat pounded in my throat. Perspiration broke out all over my body even though the whirring ceiling fans overhead cooled the air. I wiped my palms on my skirt.

Never let the monster see you sweat.

Before I could say anything, he drew me in for a kiss. Fear transformed into lust. My pulse traveled from my throat and settled between my thighs.

"How…?"

"We've established that you like vampires and werewolves. How do you feel about fallen angels?"

The crows were perched in the tree again. Carefully, I touched his skin where they landed, and explored the canvas of his flesh. My hand continued south, but stopped at the border where skin met fabric.

He undid his top button and guided my hand down the front of his trousers.

"Do angels have…?"

"I'm a *fallen* angel. We're built for sin."

He slid his pants down past his thighs, and despite the innumerable red flags, I straddled his lap.

Temporarily, I came to my senses. "What if someone sees us?"

"Let them watch," he said.

He grasped my hair in his fist, pulled my head back, and gently bit the soft flesh of my throat. The bite intensified. He drew blood and lapped at it with his rough tongue that reminded me of a cat's. He tore my panties with one forceful tug, and I bit down on my lower lip when he impaled me. Neither of us tried to steal the other's spotlight; we shared the labor and rode each other at a gentle gallop.

He hadn't told me his name, but as my excitement built, a chorus of voices whispered it inside my head.

"Kael," I moaned as a tidal wave of pleasure crashed through me.

He held my body tight to his as the last tremors of his own climax shuddered through his strong, slender form. Tears streamed down my cheeks and I moaned again as I crushed my mouth to his.

"I think you do like fallen angels," he said, and licked a trickle of blood from my neck.

"Kael. Is that your name?"

He raised a finger to his lips. "I don't want anyone else to know it. Names have power. People can use that power against you."

"Do fallen angels have wings?"

His taut belly rippled with laughter. “Yes, but not like you imagine them to be.”

I pictured Tilda Swinton as the Archangel Gabriel in *Constantine* before she lost the fight with Lucifer. Kael’s wings were probably more like a bat’s after his fall from Heaven. The thought of him standing over me with them spread at full span quickened my pulse. Excited and scared, I longed to see his true form.

I wanted more of him, but the flutter of crows’ wings beneath my fingertips snapped me out of my perverse thoughts. “Why did you sit next to me at the bar?”

He smiled and took a drag of a cigarette I hadn’t seen him light. “Loneliness is an aphrodisiac for the Fallen. I couldn’t help myself.”

“You pitied me?”

“It doesn’t sound romantic when you say it like that.”

I took a hefty pull from my fourth Manhattan. “How long have you been following me?”

“I heard you crying in the bathroom at the last bar.”

“Were you listening to me argue with my boss?”

“You mean that complete waste of a perfectly good meat sack?”

I almost laughed. “Jimmy’s chock full of icky negative feelings. Why didn’t you follow him instead?”

“His thighs don’t look as nice as yours do in a skirt.”

He licked at the trickle of blood that slowly dried under my chin and grasped my hips roughly to pull me closer.

“You taste really good. There’s something different about you. I’m eager to show you new depths of perversion, but I don’t want to wear down your batteries all at once.”

Was Kael gaining sustenance from me? Was he draining sexual energy from me like an incubus? Would he keep feeding off me until I had nothing left to give? I enjoyed his attention, but I didn’t want to die for it.

“What you’re taking from me isn’t enough, is it?”

He stopped biting my neck. “What do you mean?”

“You need more than blood and sexual energy, don’t you?”

“Yes, but I don’t want to hurt you. I’m having too much fun.”

"So, what do fallen angels eat?"

"Souls."

Fear regained its foothold over lust. "How often do you feed?"

A devious grin spread across his handsome face. "As often as possible, but I don't usually play with my food."

Being compared to an entrée made me feel less sexy. "Maybe we should get dressed."

Sitting on his lap had felt good, but thoughts of dying in his arms made me nauseous. He pulled up his pants, and then smoothed my skirt down over my legs. If anyone noticed us fucking at the back of the bar, they had kept their mouths shut.

He offered me his hand. "Shall we go hunting?"

Unless he planned on renting a boat and heading to the swamps, he didn't mean hunting for alligators.

He sensed my hesitation. "I'm not going to pretend to be something else now that you know what I am. Besides, if I'm not mistaken, knowing what I am is a kink for you."

I considered running, but knew he'd never let me go. He'd revealed himself to me. That knowledge was dangerous. "Are you going to kill me?"

He held the door open for me when we headed back out into the Quarter. "Not if you're a good girl," he said and smacked my ass.

We found Jimmy where I'd left him, harassing a couple of twenty-something bimbos. The girls were glad for the interruption.

Jimmy was surprised to see me and looked nervous as he pointed at Kael with his chin. "Who's this?"

"A friend."

They shook hands, but I didn't introduce them. Kael went to order drinks, leaving me alone with Jimmy.

"Look, I'm really sorry about how I treated you earlier. Are we cool?" He had to shout over the music.

"It doesn't matter," I said.

"Of course it matters. We're friends and I treated you like shit."

"Seriously, don't worry about it."

He grasped my arm hard enough to make me wince. "Where did you find the stiff in the suit?"

"He stalked me to a bar over on Frenchman."

"You're kidding, right?"

Kael returned with our drinks. He leaned over so that Jimmy and I could hear him. "She's not kidding. Initially, I was just going to suck out her soul and throw her husk in a dumpster. Then we started talking and once I had a taste of her, I figured there was more between us than just à la carte." Kael laughed at the look on Jimmy's face. "You really should have tasted her when you had the chance."

Jimmy wasn't laughing.

I sipped my drink and Kael wrapped his arm around my waist. He smelled my hair, kissed the top of my head, and then pulled me tight up against him.

Jimmy stared at us with his mouth slightly open before finding his voice. "Seriously, who is this guy?"

"I'm the best fuck this gorgeous creature's had in a long time. What the hell were you waiting for? She was practically straight out of the package fresh." Kael sniffed his fingers and licked the tips.

Jimmy's hands clenched into fists. "Do you kiss your mother with that mouth?"

"No, but I'll be sure to kiss your wife when I see her in Hell," Kael said.

Jimmy glared at me. "Is that supposed to be funny?"

Kael sniffed the air inches from Jimmy's face and licked his lips. "You are a smorgasbord of emotional delights—fear, sorrow, rage, and now jealousy. Why?"

"That's none of your fucking business." Jimmy turned his attention back to me. "What have you been telling this guy?"

"He overheard our fight earlier. And I think he can read our minds," I said with a shrug.

"This isn't funny anymore. I told you I'm sorry. You can accept my apology or not." He turned to walk away. Kael grabbed his shoulder and whispered in his ear. All the color drained from Jimmy's face. "How do you know my wife's name?"

"I told you, she's in Hell," Kael said. "She died an hour ago."

Jimmy looked like someone had punched him in the gut. Asshole or not, he was in pain.

A tear trickled down Jimmy's cheek. "She's really dead?"

"Yes, and now you have nothing to live for. Which works out for both of us, because I'm going to eat your soul."

Jimmy's body shook with sobs as we escorted him out of the bar. "Did she suffer?"

"No, she died in her sleep," Kael said.

Jimmy turned to me. "Is he telling the truth?"

"It's what you want to hear, isn't it?"

He nodded and wiped his nose on his shirtsleeve.

Once we were outside, Kael slammed Jimmy against a brick wall and ripped into his throat. A spray of arterial blood splattered Kael's pale face before he pressed his mouth against the wound. I knew I should look away, but I couldn't.

The rusted iron scent of Jimmy's blood competed with the stink of garbage in the alley, making me gag. When he finished, Kael lifted Jimmy's body over his head as if he weighed nothing, and then threw him in the dumpster. He turned to fix his gaze on me like he was about to feed again. Inky black replaced the icy blue and white of his eyes.

I slowly backed away until I hit the brick wall of the alley. Could I run fast enough to get away from him if he decided he was still hungry?

"Don't run. If I wanted to kill you, you'd never get away." His voice was husky. Languid. Deep red stained his cheeks and mouth, and blood dripped from his chin, ruining his white shirt.

My breath came in short rapid bursts. I had watched Kael kill Jimmy and did nothing to stop him. Yes, I was afraid of Kael, but my attraction to him clouded my fear. I wanted to taste his mouth again.

Feel his hands on my body even though they were covered in Jimmy's blood. Kael was right. Fear was my kink and I was trembling all over.

Did my desires make me more of a monster than Kael?

He hung his jacket over the side of a dumpster before removing his bloodstained shirt. He used it like a napkin, and then he tossed it in the dumpster with Jimmy's body. He put his jacket back on, quieting the crows squawking and flapping their wings across his chest.

"You're exciting them with your fear," he whispered against my ear.

Back inside the bar, I sat on a wooden bench enclosed by a metal cage and tried to light a cigarette. My hands were shaking, and I couldn't make the lighter work. Jimmy was dead. The creature that killed him brought me my sixth Manhattan.

"You're upset. We should go," he said.

My instincts told me to run, but I knew my efforts would be pointless.

He offered me his hand and led me out of the bar to a waiting cab. He told the driver to take us to Metairie.

"What address?" The driver's Middle Eastern accent was heavy.

"You can drop us near the cemetery," Kael said.

"The cemeteries are dangerous at night," the driver said.

Kael laughed and handed the driver a fifty-dollar bill before sliding his hand beneath my skirt. His mouth covered my gasp, and his caresses worked me into a feverish state. He parted my knees and buried his face between my thighs. A voice in the back of my head told me to make him stop. I ignored it. My eyes fluttered closed and I dug my heels into the back of the front seat as I shouted his name. I looked up in time to see the driver staring at me in the rearview mirror. Embarrassed, I looked away. Kael bit into my thigh and lapped at the blood. Little sips of my soul.

He raised his head from my lap. His eyes were black bottomless pits. I shivered and his smile widened.

The cab slowed down. Kael climbed back onto the seat. My blood stained his mouth. The driver gave a start when he glanced into his rearview mirror again. He murmured something under his breath.

"Pray all you like, but Allah isn't listening," Kael said and opened the car door.

"Miss, please. I will take you anywhere you want to go. No charge. You shouldn't be left alone with this man." The driver's voice shook.

Kael offered the driver more money. The denominations must have eased his worries, because he drove off and never looked back.

The cemetery gates opened at a wave of Kael's hand. I followed him until he stopped before a large, alabaster mausoleum with an inscription above the arch.

Sic itur ad astra.

"I never bothered learning Latin. What does it mean?"

He laughed. "Thus, do we reach the stars."

He waved his hand again, and a portal appeared in the sealed doorway of the tomb. He grasped my wrist and pulled me through. I'm not sure what I expected, but the passage from the cemetery lawn into the antechamber of the tomb was uneventful. Flickering torches lighted the granite walls and cast shadows into the entryway that led to a room furnished with a couch, two chairs, and a bookcase filled with ancient and modern tomes. Next to the bookcase was a liquor cabinet. He offered to fix me a drink.

"I've had six Manhattans this evening. I'm surprised I'm still standing."

He gathered me up in his arms and carried me to a chamber beyond the sitting room. Candelabra of varying shapes and sizes dripped wax from burning candles. A king-sized bed adorned with black velvet drapes occupied the center of the room. An open book and a half-full bottle of wine along with an empty glass sat on the marble-topped nightstand.

I ruffled his hair and bit his earlobe.

He stroked my face with the back of his hand. "Undress me."

I obeyed his command. My hands clasped behind his neck to draw him closer so that I could taste his mouth. I lingered there for a few moments, and then let my tongue glide down to his collarbone. As I kissed his throat and upper chest, I slipped his jacket off his shoulders and let it fall to the floor. I caressed his bare arms and placed gentle kisses on each one before I tortured his nipples with my tongue and teeth. He grasped my hips roughly and turned me around. My breath caught in my throat as he lifted my skirt. I willed myself to stop swaying in time with the motion of his hips and spun to face him again.

"Don't…" he stuttered.

He fell silent as I unfastened his trousers and slowly lowered them to the floor. Kneeling before him, my nails traced deep scratches along the backs of his thighs as I guided him into my mouth. A shudder ran through him as he resisted the urge to thrust his hips forward. I ripped deep, panting moans from him, and my own arousal intensified.

He stopped me. "I want more than just your mouth." He bent me over the mattress and plowed into me, making me gasp.

"You like the way I fuck you, don't you?"

"Yes," I panted.

"You're mine now."

I didn't care about the consequences of belonging to this monster. Deep shudders racked my body as he brought me closer to climax. Before either of us could finish, he stopped.

"No…." I pleaded and reached for him.

He slapped my hand playfully and produced an ancient-looking tattoo needle and bottle of black ink from the nightstand drawer. He dipped the needle into the dark liquid and sketched a design at the base of my spine.

Panic made my heart thunder in my chest. "Wait, what are you…?"

"Hush," he said.

Small barbs lined the surface of the instrument that bit into my sensitive skin. Pain made my back arch like a cat's, but his eager caresses between my thighs kept my mind focused on the pleasure and I relaxed. The needle burned an image, or was it a word, into my flesh. Without seeing the design, I knew it was his name.

Blood and sweat mixed with ink, stinging the invisible cuts in my skin. He set aside the bottle and needle and entered me forcefully. I gripped the sheets as he rode me like a wild beast. He was the Big Bad Wolf, growling, grunting, and panting as he ruined me for all other lovers to come.

"Oh fuck!" His hips snapped forward and he finally let go. I was conscious long enough to feel him caress my breasts and kiss the back of my neck.

When I awoke my cheek rested on a satin pillow, but my wrists and ankles were shackled, and my rear end was raised in the air. I tried to move to get a better look at my surroundings. Kael sat in a chair across the room. He was still naked and his vulture-like wings, darker than midnight, were unfurled around his muscular shoulders. A book balanced on his abdomen and he appeared to be deep in thought. He took off his glasses when he saw that I was awake.

"You don't have to chain me to keep me here."

"I know, but it's more fun this way."

He smacked my ass then rubbed the sting away. I felt a gentle gust of air as his powerful wings spread open to their full span. He looked more like a bird of prey than the bat I'd imagined. The feathers tickled my bare skin as he bent to kiss my flesh where he had engraved his name. Just as I relaxed, he smacked my ass hard three more times. Tears sprang to my eyes, but I knew not to ask him to stop. When he eased the pain this time, his fingers explored hidden parts of me and confirmed my arousal.

"I knew you were a bad girl; you want to be punished," he whispered against my ear.

I sighed.

"Are you thirsty?"

I nodded.

He brought me water and told me to lap it from the palm of his hand. The idea of becoming his pet filled me with terror and set my libido on fire. How long would I be chained to his bed? What if he grew bored of this game? I knew too much about him. I thought of Jimmy lying dead in the alley.

Eventually Kael would need something more from me. How long would my body be able to endure his version of affection?

Kael's strong hands caressed my back, breasts, abdomen, and thighs, and brought me back to the present. His touch was more like an acolyte's than a lover's. He was worshipping my body, appraising it, learning all of its secrets through his probing fingertips.

"I want you," he sighed.

"Take me," I moaned and fought against my restraints to get closer to him.

"So eager to please me, so willing to give." He chuckled and continued exploring every inch of my flesh.

"Anything," I whispered.

"Anything?"

"Yes."

"I thought this body was made for sin, but your body is a temple to lust," he grunted, entering me.

He churned inside me, taking his time, touching, teasing, and tasting me. My mind swam with images of crows in flight—their wings beating against a dark sky in an ecstatic state until they landed on a pyramid of corpses. Men and women, all beautiful, all naked, all dead. I didn't recognize any of them. They were all strangers to me except for one. Near the top of the death mound was Kael, but he wasn't dead. His face was contorted into a mask of agony and ecstasy, as if he were on the verge of experiencing the most pleasurable and painful orgasm of his life. Was I seeing one of Kael's memories, or was it his fantasy? I tried to get a closer look at him, but the vision faded when I felt the manacles holding my wrists and ankles unlock.

Kael climbed onto the bed and lay down next to me. He took my hands and helped me straddle his waist, reigniting my flame with his skillful touch.

"Let me look at you," he said.

I knew very little about religion, but the look on his face was unmistakable even to a layperson. He was in the throes of religious fervor. Curses and expletives erupted from his mouth as if he were speaking in tongues.

"Say my name." He covered my breast with an open mouth kiss.

His stamina was infectious. The motion of our bodies moving in time together energized me. I threw my head back and shouted his name. "Kael."

The base of my spine tingled, a tiny stab of pain from where the needle had carved his sacred graffiti.

He flipped me over and drove himself into me again. My legs rested against his chest, my feet dangling in the air above me.

"Say it again," he growled.

Every part of me hummed and trembled as I drew closer to my climax. He kept it at bay, prolonging the payoff for both of us.

"Kael," I panted.

Another sharp pain. A jolt of electricity spread from my tailbone, ran along my spine, and ended at the base of my skull. Heat blanketed my body, like a fever.

"You feel it, don't you," he whispered.

I nodded. I'd never felt such intense pleasure before. It was maddening. If fucking Kael meant losing my mind, I was ready to live in an asylum.

"Again, say my name again." His wings stirred the air around us in a spastic frenzy as he succumbed to his release. The birds on his chest joined the frantic dance. Dark feathers floated around me and landed on my face and breasts and caught in my hair.

"Kael," I screamed. The tattoo at the base of my spine exploded with pain as bright as a dying star. He collapsed on top of me, his face peaceful and serene. It was the last thing I saw.

I'm not sure how long I was asleep. Minutes? Hours? It varies from body to body. The dead man's skin was cold against mine. His cock was still stiff and that zealous grin remained plastered across his handsome face. I shoved him off me onto the floor and almost wished he'd survived the ritual. They rarely did. Too bad, it would be nice to enjoy his body from the outside again. But once I possessed a new body, the old one was useless. It seemed like such a terrible waste.

This new body was stronger. I had been right, there was something different about her. She had even seen the graveyard of souls in my mind. Whatever she was, she was mine now.

I stepped over the dead man to admire my new body in the mirror and felt a stab of . . . what? Guilt? No, never guilt. Loss. He really had been beautiful. My kin wouldn't have been put off by the fact that he was dead. They would have enjoyed his body one last time. Not me. I prefer sex with the living. The dead don't weep or beg for mercy when you torture them.

REMEMBER ME

by
EV Knight

The Moore house? Shit.

Sam's stomach twisted, threatening a bout of diarrhea. Why him? Mac knew how Sam felt about that place. A cool waft of air brushed the back of his sweaty neck and ruffled the yellowed, curling newspaper clippings that hung beside the daily work-order assignment sheet. The little black oscillating fan worked well enough to keep the dust in the air instead of settling on the old seventies vinyl furniture. One would think a guy who advertised his business as "Mac of All Trades" could install air conditioning in the damned office trailer.

Sam stabbed his finger to still the small rectangle of paper wagging back and forth in a "you can't catch me" tease. His friend's face stared at him beneath the headline:

Missing
Adrien Comstock, Age 19.

"You ought to be taking this one with me, dickhead," he said. "Missing, my ass. You took off and left me in this shithole. Now I gotta go up there and deal with that old bat alone."

Adrien wasn't the only young adult male to go missing from the town. Hadn't anyone noticed that guys his age took off all the time? Nobody wanted to get stuck in this dead-end town, but they didn't want to live the college life either. It was easier to bail than face their blue-collar parents' disapproval.

He guessed he was lucky to have done well at the Vo-Tech to get this job at Mac's. There weren't many options in Carlton. Sam wasn't surprised Adrien ran off, but it would have been nice for Adrien to invite him along.

"Hey, Mac, what's the psycho up on the hill want this time?" he yelled, leaning back to peek into the boss's office

"Probably got another notice from the city to clean it up or else. She said something about the pool too," Mac said from behind a newspaper and a puff of cigar smoke. Only in Carlton could a man like Mac still sit at a desk barking orders from behind a real-life newspaper. He probably had a phone book in his metal desk drawer too.

"I ain't no pool guy."

"Just get your ass up there. We don't turn down a job, you know that."

"Place is fuckin' creepy, Mac. She's fuckin' creepy."

"She's just a lonely ol' woman stuck in that big-ass house. Give her a break and clean the pool out."

Sam waved a dismissing hand and started for the door.

"And take one of those respirator masks, I've heard stories."

"Yeah, me too," Sam said, shoving a couple in his bag.

Plenty of stories. Once upon a time, a glittering mansion, owned by a mining tycoon and his wife, sat on a hill overlooking the village of Carlton. The tales of glorious Christmas parties and summer barbecues held for the miners and their families contrasted to the ones told by Sam and his friends. Things had changed between the days their grandparents enjoyed shrimp cocktail on the patio and the eighties when the industry decline put many men out of work. When Henry Moore disappeared ten years ago, rumors about Judy and her mental health supplied the perfect fodder with which pre-teen boys could scare the shit out of each other.

The ride through town exemplified on a larger scale what happened to the Moores. The drab colors and abandoned storefronts depressed Sam. Everything seemed so much brighter in his memories. Carlton sat on a muddy branch of the Susquehanna reflecting the river back on itself rather than the other way around. At least Stucky's was still booming. Every town like this needed a good dive bar and Stucky's had offered that service for at least thirty years.

Maybe he'd stop in on the way back, have a cold one before going back to whatever mundane tasks awaited him at Mac's.

Sam let the truck idle at the entrance to the drive. He wasn't scared, he told himself. It was just that he hadn't been on this property in almost ten years. The blanched skin overlying his knuckles belied his self-assurances. Ten years, and yet the memory of that night with Adrien was as sharp as if it happened yesterday. The fear, the gut-wrenching discovery, followed by the admonitions of their parents and mockery from their peers, had left an emotional scar that never healed.

It had been Labor Day weekend, the last days of freedom before school. Earlier that year, Henry Moore just sort of disappeared. No one saw him around town anymore. Judy began calling for grocery delivery and handyman services. The talk in town was that he'd run off with the bulk of their money, pushing Judy further into a psychosis that had always been simmering under the surface, if the rumors were to be believed.

When most boys were out at the baseball field hitting pop-up flies, Adrien and Sam were reading Stephen King and Dean Koontz. With a predisposition for the creepy unknown, they'd managed, over the course of the summer, to convince themselves that Crazy Judy was a witch who had chopped up her husband into pieces and fed him to the German Pointers Henry had kept as hunting dogs.

It took super sleuths like Adrien and Sam to piece together the overheard conversations of retired miners in the barbershop and their wives at the laundromat. Adrien kept a notebook with words like "man-eater" underlined. Direct quotes that bolstered their theories were always attributed for potential interviews at a later date.

"Well, I for one would never let Jim go to that house alone. Never trusted that woman. I might not see him again."—*Jennifer Ames, husband worked at mine. Daughter Lily in 10th grade*

"It's no wonder Henry took off, he was probably sick and tired of tripping over other men just to get to his bedroom."—*Mike Douglass, worked at mine. No kids*

Sam chuckled nervously and rubbed the sweat of his palms on his jeans. They'd just misunderstood the unspoken meaning in the gossip. That's all. So why wasn't he getting out of the truck? Because he wasn't convinced that he and Adrien were wrong. Because deep down inside there was a little boy convinced that the woman was crazy enough to kill a man … or two.

The thing was, after Henry took off, Judy took to wearing black Victorian mourning dresses and blond wigs in 1950s pinup style. The grass grew high and wild. The hunting dogs left their outdoor kennels for the luxury of indoor living. Their cages rusted, patio furniture that tipped over during storms was never righted, and the occasional lawn tractor would, for unknown reasons, be abandoned in the yard.

Gradually, the once "Crown of the Town" became a junkyard glaring down on the city, daring anyone to complain. Occasionally, Judy would be seen outside, walking through her rust kingdom, black umbrella in hand to ward off the sun. For ten-year-old boys it was the final nail in the coffin of determining that she was, indeed, a witch.

It was here, where Sam's truck sat idling, that they stopped and left their bikes. The trees at the end of the driveway provided good cover. It was great to hide bikes then and it was a good place to sit in a truck trying to find the guts to face ten years' worth of childish fears.

"Okay, we flip for it," Adrien said, digging in the pocket of his shorts.

"Heads," Sam called. It was heads.

"Shit."

"Yes!" Sam cheered himself. "Okay, so you have to go up there and look in the windows, the *back* windows, and then you have to walk through the junk pile and back down here." Sam was all about the plan now that he was off the hook.

"Fine, but you still have to be a lookout, and if she comes out you have to distract her. That's the deal."

"Yeah, yeah, just go, before she turns all the lights out." Sam nudged Adrien, who wiped the new sweat off his forehead and headed up the drive on the far side of the bushes.

Sam watched his friend disappear into the shadows. He waited in the cool summer dusk, which gradually became a cloudy summer night. He watched for fireflies but they'd gone wherever they go at the end of summer. He kicked gravel into speed bumps for ants. Where was Adrien? Even in kid-time, where a minute was an hour, it had been too long.

A chicken would have grabbed his bike and headed home to get grown-up help, but Sam was no chicken. He dragged their bikes off the road and onto the embankment and then headed straight up the driveway. Witch be damned, he was going to get his friend back.

"Excuse me, ma'am, sorry to bother you but my friend came up here to ask you about a fundraiser for school and I must have missed him coming back down, has he been here yet?" he whispered, practicing his cover in case she discovered him lurking about her house.

Without the headlight of his bike, all he could see were monstrous black outlines in the backyard of what was maybe an old tractor but that also could have been a giant mutant waiting to devour him. As he approached the house, Sam inched closer to its outer walls. Three sides vulnerable was better than four. Although the closer he crept, the stronger the faint smell of decay became.

"Yuck."

Sam rounded the corner of the house into the back yard, which was littered with rusty outdoor furniture, ripped and bent umbrellas, and various motorized contraptions in different states of decay. From the light from a single window, he could easily see that none of them were ancient giant creatures waiting to devour him.

"Adrien," he whisper-shouted. "Where are you? Let's go."

The silence was broken by the lapping of water on the sides of the in-ground pool. Oh, God, please don't let him be drowned. Sam left the protection of the house and ventured slowly to the edge of the tiled deck. The thudding in his chest sounded like footsteps on the patio. Someone coming to push him in with the other bodies floating in it. And there was indeed a lot of shit bobbing on the surface. Sam stepped closer to the edge in order to better see the flotsam.

"Go! Go, go, go!" Adrien shoved him.

Sam jumped and lost his footing. His right leg slipped over the lip of the deck and broke through the scummy skin on the surface of the water.

"Ugh! Oh shit!" he yelled.

"Shhh, shhh. She'll hear you," Adrien said. He grabbed Sam's arms and dragged him out of the pool.

"Come on, we gotta get out of here."

The rough edge of the patio scraped his belly. "Oh man, it stinks so bad," he said, standing up with his wet leg and shoe raised. Adrien shoved him again.

"Go! She's a murderer! I saw him, I saw his body. And she saw me! Run!"

They went straight to the police department. The cops humored the boys, scolded them for trespassing, called their parents, and promised they'd send someone to check it out. The boys got grounded and the only thing Judy got was a notice to clean up her yard. At school, it was worse. No one believed them, and they called them the Winchester Boys for the next few years.

Still, it *was* creepy, and Judy Moore was obviously off her rocker. But she must be in her seventies now—what could she possibly do to him? He just needed to get his ass up there, deal with her nasty cesspool, and praise the Lord that he didn't have to do anything more than that. The yard looked more like a public garbage dump in the middle of a junkyard. He studied the layout of the trash-field he would have to traverse to get to the pool.

He took a deep breath, grabbed his tool box, and snapped a respirator mask on his head for use when he got closer. In his childhood, the house had towered over him. Now, it sat humbled. Its peeling paint left a depressed gray in its wake. Where there had once been a stone paved walk to the front door was now a jungle of weeds, as if someone inside was losing a game of Jumanji. Well, he wasn't in the mood for playing games. As it was, this whole house call felt like a gamble.

Making it to the front porch with only a few scratches to show for it, Sam rang the bell. It took forever for her to answer. See, he assured himself, the woman was old, frail, and slow—no danger here. The door opened as slowly as it had taken her to get there in the first place.

There was a reason for that, and it wasn't age. It was the massive pile of filth she was pulling the door against. A peek into the house revealed a room piled with newspapers and magazines, plastic bowls, and dog shit. The stink that rushed out at him made him retch. He swallowed against it and smiled.

"Hello, Mrs. Moore. I'm here to look at your pool."

She stepped into the open space, blocking his view of the room beyond. The wrinkled, aged face beneath the platinum-blond wig reminded him of an old black-and-white movie starring Bette Davis as a crazy old rich woman suspected of killing her fiancé years before. Gone, though, was the mourning dress. Today Judy was wearing a low-cut black jumpsuit and leopard-print slippers.

"Oh, thank goodness," she said. "I can't take it anymore. I'm sure the filter is clogged up with something and now the whole pool is filthy. And the odor—I have to warn you young man, the smell is just rancid." She rubbed her hands together in front of her like a spider.

He bit his lip. If a woman who was living in an atmosphere of rotting meat thought the pool smelled bad, he was fucked.

"Well, sounds like we better take a look. Is there a way to get to the pool from inside the house?" It was morbid curiosity, true, but more so, a straight path to the pool through a roomful of trash was better than the field of tetanus out back.

"No, honey, I'm sorry. I haven't had a chance to pick up, and the dogs are hungry." She smiled. Her teeth were stained brown.

Sam nodded, fearing if he spoke, a throat spasm would betray his disgust.

"Okay then, if you can show me the best way to, uh, get there," he said, turning around as if just now noticing the mess outside.

"Just follow the house around to the back. The pool's there, you can't miss it. There is a shed on the far side of it. The filter is under its flooring."

The hair tingled on the back of his neck. He'd be retracing his steps from a decade before.

Grow up, he scolded himself, and headed that way.

"The shed back there has some chemicals still in it, if you don't mind throwing them in when you've fixed the filter. I've been thinking about using it for water aerobics," she called out.

Maybe she ought to clean the place up as exercise first. He rolled his eyes and headed to the pool. The savannah of weeds hid all sorts of hazards, but he followed the swampy smell and soon an oval of shit-brown water appeared like an anti-oasis in the center of the rusty grasslands.

The thick, rank air around the pool stunk of organic decomposition with an acrid ghost just beneath it.

"Jesus Christ," Sam said. "There's gotta be some dead animal rotting in there."

He glanced in the pool as he walked toward the shed. Gray lumps of God-knows-what bobbed on the murky surface, occasionally tearing away at the pudding skin that had formed around them. He could almost taste the reek coming up off the water. It burnt his tongue as well as his nostrils. Sam pulled the respirator mask down.

The shed was a cool reprieve, and surprisingly tidy. He shut the door and took deep, cleansing breaths through the respirator. His eyes adjusted to the dark. Everything he suspected he would need was in here. He grabbed a bottle of shock down from the shelf hanging beside what looked like a gun rack which held the pool vac and skimming net.

A rattle beneath a wooden door in the floor sent vibrations to his feet. He pulled it up. The struggling filter had its own odor—hot, as if the motor was burning. Sam lifted the lid and gagged. Sludge that resembled toddler snot lay on the bottom of an otherwise waterless well.

"Shit," he muttered.

The clog was back at the intake inside the pool. He dropped the filter door and grabbed the net off the rack. If he was lucky, he could use it to dislodge whatever it was instead of having to reach into the pool—or worse—get into it. He took two more deep breaths of stale air and walked back out to the pool.

Down on his knees, Sam pushed the skimmer net into the filthy water. It scraped against something stuck over the intake filter. It was heavy, whatever it was, and he couldn't seem to dislodge it. His nose stung, even with the respirator, which seemed to be doing nothing but causing claustrophobia. He ripped it off and tossed it away.

He tried the net again but still could not free the blockage. On a whim, he swept it along the bottom and brought it to the surface.

It held fleshy, pale pink fragments of what could have been some aquatic fungus, but what did he know? And now there were new, huge holes in the netting allowing most of his catch to fall through. Probably a dead animal in the pool. That would explain the brown scum on the top of the water as well as the weight ripping the net. It was probably a deer, or maybe a dog.

"Fuck," he muttered and plunged his hand into the water up to his shoulder. His fingers brushed against the blockage. Whatever it was felt gooey and there was hair. Long hair. A dog then. He grabbed it and pulled hard. Just it detached, his skin began to itch. Sam hefted the thing out of the water and stared at what remained of a human head.

Half the face appeared to have melted off. The remaining eyeball was milky and shriveled. Much of the boney side had also been dissolved away, and the spongy, honeycombed inside was exposed. In other areas, like the empty eye socket, there was just a hole. It was probably his imagination again, what with this whole day screaming déjà vu, but what was left of the features on the head looked like Adrien.

A burning pain worked its way up his arm and he dropped the head. It hit the stone deck flesh side down, but instead of rolling, it just splattered and stuck where it fell. Sam felt his gorge rise in his throat but the stinging in his arm overrode any other thought. The skin on his arm tingled and turned white. Tiny bubbles erupted from his own flesh. He hugged his arm close against himself and bent around it protectively.

"I truly miss having so many young men around the house. Oh, the parties we used to throw. 'Course, Henry never cared for the way I entertained his employees." Judy's voice so close behind him made him jump.

Before he could move she had his hair in her hand and shoved his face into the water. The pain was breathtaking. He closed his eyes a second too late. They burned in their sockets. Instinctively, he opened his mouth to scream. It filled with water that tasted like aspirin soaked in vinegar. She pulled him back up and out. He scrambled backward like a crab, away from the water, spitting out the noxious stuff.

"Nowadays, you can't trust a man to keep secrets. I forgave you two when you were kids up here spying on me."

The world was a blur, cloudy and dim. His skin sizzled. Sam could make out the shape of the pool and recalled the sliding glass doors into the house just across from where he stood. If he could get in, wash his face and rinse his eyes, he might be able to get to the hospital on his own.

The psychotic old woman was still talking about parties and men and Adrien.

"I need to get to a hospital. My arm, my face." It was all he could say. His tongue felt three sizes too big for his mouth.

"Oh yes, it's the hydrogen fluoride I put in the water. I was hoping it was concentrated enough to eat him all up, but he just clogged the filter. So, now I have *two* pool boys to dispose of."

Sam stumbled to his feet, finding his balance. He staggered toward the doors. He needed water, had to wash this stuff off. Using his good left hand, he managed to pull the door open.

Inside was no less nauseating than the pool, and the darkness made his visual acuity so much worse. He stepped toward what looked like the vague outline of a kitchen sink and fell into a mass of empty milk jugs and yogurt containers.

Judy followed him, chatting all the while. "I'll take care of you as soon as the dogs are fed. Poor things were only puppies when Henry left us. They never learned to hunt their food properly."

Sam heard her slide the door shut and then whistle. He scrambled to his feet and made a lunge at the sink and swiped away whatever trash was piled up in front of the faucets. The thunderous sound of at least three, maybe four large dogs tearing through piles of trash in the house didn't help his blind search for aquatic salvation.

The first bite stopped him from any further searching. The dogs ruthlessly tore into his legs and one jumped up and caught purchase of his T-shirt.

"Were my babies hungry? Were they?" Judith was asking them somewhere in the back of the madness that filled his head.

He yelled as he kicked the dogs off. *Run, just run. Get out of the house and scream for help as best you can.* Blood trickled down his leg and he suspected that his run would be more of a fast limp, but he had to try. Had to get out.

Judy blocked the sliding door he had come in through and the dogs stood guard at the archway between the kitchen and the living room, waiting for Judy's command. If he couldn't escape, he'd need to get away and find a phone. He brought his shirt up to wipe off his face and eyes. It hurt to rub them, and it didn't help anyway. His vision was fucked. The dogs had come from a hallway to his right. If he charged that way, pushing as much trash down behind him as he went, he might buy himself some time. He launched himself in that direction, hoping for enough sensory input to find help.

A room was open at the end of the hall. He could make out the white door open at an angle and a glow of light inside. A bedroom, most likely. She was old. He gambled that there might be a phone on the nightstand.

The dogs barked behind him, working their way over the precarious obstacle course of plastic and paper. The floor in front of the door became swampy and the raw sewage stink worked its way into his already damaged lungs. He heaved his breakfast onto the floor. It faded right into the rest of the muck.

Black garbage bags stood sentry on either side of the doorway, leaving a narrow space to squeeze through. Sam shoved them behind him, ignoring it when his skin stuck to the plastic. His leg dripped blood and his arm seeped clear watery blister juice so that his whole body felt cold, wet, and sticky all at the same time. His foot caught on something poking out of the top bag and he fell forward, rolling into the room.

Here the smell was mustier and a dehumidifier hummed from somewhere in the room. But its purr wasn't enough to draw Sam's attention away from the bed, where he could make out the outline of a body lying stiffly on its back.

"Guh," he said.

It could be a mannequin, but he had a feeling that if he reached out and touched it, it would feel mummified. Like a body that had been lying on this bed, in this room, for ten years. A body that a little boy saw lying here when he looked through a window that many years ago.

"It was nice of you to run in here like that," Judy said. "It's getting harder for me to drag the bodies. That's how your friend ended up in the pool. I slipped and he fell right in."

Dogs panted behind her. He heard them better than he could see them. Their dark coats blended against the black trash bags. There was no way out of this room. He turned back to the far side where light streamed through a window. He'd have to break through it. But then, on the nightstand, the light touched a square white object that could be a phone. He'd have to crawl overtop the body on the bed, but what choice did he have now?

He stepped. The floor rolled out from under him and he fell. His arm was on fire, skin torn off like a stewed tomato.

The dogs whimpered anxiously. Judy stepped into the room.

"I really only wanted to keep Henry with me. He didn't like the mess and threatened to leave me. I couldn't have that."

Her leopard slippers made a squishing sound when she stepped. She pushed a path in the long, rounded objects that scattered the floor. He managed to get one with his still functioning hand to use as a weapon. This close, he could identify the items surrounding him. It was bones he'd slipped on. Many in different states of decay. Some had bits of old meat still attached and most had teeth marks from the dogs, who clearly spent much of their time in this room.

"The problem was, the dogs just wouldn't leave him be. They were just always at him."

He couldn't slither under the bed because there was a body occupying the space. He couldn't die here, not like this, not at the hands of a crazy old witch.

She inched closer. The phone was so far away.

"I needed to feed them, but after they'd had a taste of Henry, well, what was I supposed to do? They didn't want dog food and I couldn't bear to have them put down."

She let him stand. The room spun, and he collapsed onto the bed. Didn't matter, he'd crawl over the fucking mummy if he had to.

"But, what with the mess outside, there is always a good Samaritan coming around offering help." Judy sat down on the corner of the bed. "And when they don't, I call for help, and they send me strapping young men." She grinned.

He could see the shadows of filth on the otherwise white teeth. An image of her sharing the feast with her dogs flashed in Sam's mind. She reached out for him, her long nails brushing against his acid-ravaged forearm.

"Don't touch me, you bitch," he tried, but it came out all mush-mouthed. "Dond dud ee, uu biish."

He had little strength left to shove her away, but he did his best. The sensation of hanging strips of flesh wiggling like cooked spaghetti as he moved made his stomach flop. Unconsciousness threatened his already clouded vision.

"Oh, my babies love tough guys like you."

The bedsprings creaked. Sam threw himself on top of the dead body on the bed.

"Henry always liked to watch," she said.

He was so close, though. He grabbed the phone and ran his hand over the buttons feeling for the nine. He had to ignore whatever it was she was doing to make the bed jiggle so much behind him. He hit the nine and searched for the one.

"It was his secret, watching. He thought I didn't know. Just like you and your friend didn't think I knew how you liked to watch."

Sam swung back around, phone in hand. He was certain he'd punched in 911. All he had to do was fend her and the dogs off until help arrived.

But Judy knelt on her knees right behind him with a big chunk of ore held over her head in weak trembling hands. He squinted, unable to focus. Dogs barked, and bones scattered in the background. A heavy thud echoed through his skull. He dropped the receiver.

"Nine-one-one, what's your emergency?" a voice buzzed in the background as Sam fought to stay conscious amidst a sea of chaos.

"Oh, my mistake, dear. So sorry to bother you," Judy said, and hung up the phone. "Henry liked to watch, but Judy likes to remember. When you remember everyone's secrets, there isn't anything you can't get away with."

The last thing Sam remembered before giving in to the darkness of the bedroom for good was Judy Moore tearing away a little piece of his flesh for herself.

DARKSIDE EFFECT

by
Serena Jayne

Every partnership requires trust, but sometimes the construction, like a house of cards, was pieced together with nothing more than hot wind on one end and desperate hope on the other.

I hurried across the college campus where I worked, dodging students and faculty alike. Maybe they were late, like me, but unlike me, their tardiness was based on their choices—clocking too many hours trying to crack another video game level, a late-night booty call, a craving for a chocolate-glazed donut from the hot new bakery across town. The illness, which stole my ability to control my body, wasn't something anyone would choose.

Yet again I'd woken helpless until I regained the strength to move my muscles. The only bright note was the lack of the hallucinations that occasionally accompanied the sleep paralysis. Most people thought narcolepsy simply made a person sleepy. My disease came with every single bell and whistle. Lucky me. I'd do anything to have a normal life.

I ducked into the laboratory I shared with my coworker Miles. Pungent chemical and biological odors made me wrinkle my nose. He spent most of his time with his blue-gloved hands shoved inside the fume hood and his nose pressed against the safety glass. But other than the mechanical sounds of myriad equipment clicking, hissing, and whirling, the laboratory was deader than the scores of rats we'd sacrificed in the name of science.

I found him hunched over his desk in our tiny office. He'd decorated his side with B-movie posters of big-busted women fleeing from zombies, space monsters, and ginormous lizards. An Elvira bobble head nodded in submission as though she considered Miles her lord and master.

Seeing my area of the office never failed to ignite a feeling of calm. All my pens and other office supplies were tucked away in drawers, leaving the surface of my desk empty and uncluttered. I'd used measuring tape to ensure the sole personal item on display, the certificate I'd received from completing a six-month self-defense program, hung perfectly centered.

I perched on the edge of Miles's desk and clutched my morning mug of rooibos tea. My brain felt fuzzy, as though Styrofoam peanuts packed my cranium. I couldn't remember the last time I'd been clearheaded or anything less than exhausted.

Miles wore the same hangdog expression as he had three months ago after I'd turned down his offer of becoming friends with benefits. When I was an undergrad, a guy from my quantitative analysis class took me out for drinks and then proceeded to take me by force. These days, the mere thought of a man's touch made my insides churn like a viscous solution inside an Erlenmeyer flask hovering over a Bunsen burner flame.

"Beth." His gaze flicked from my chest to my eyes and then back down again. "Three more rejection letters arrived in interoffice mail."

"We'd have plenty of funding if KZ-9608 combatted male pattern baldness or guaranteed the subject an erection or cured herpes or one of those colored-ribbon diseases." I set my mug on a pile of notebooks and buttoned up my lab coat.

"Seemed best to focus on rare illnesses to take advantage of the orphan drug regulations. Helping your condition is an added perk." He sniffed at my drink, scrunched up his face, and pushed the mug away as though the contents were poisoned. "Maybe if you weren't a tea freak, you wouldn't be narcoleptic."

Refusing to defend my hatred for all things coffee yet again, I raised my eyebrows. If we had data supporting the safety and efficacy of the drug in primates, the sky would rain grant money for clinical trials.

"Sucks to give up on the project without knowing if we're on the right track."

Sucks to abandon the pursuit of a new narcolepsy treatment. Sucks to be a slave to my stupid affliction.

Drugs didn't cure most diseases. The best hope was to find something to merely manage the symptoms. Symptoms which were slowly destroying my life.

I was worn down by the sleep paralysis, muscle weakness, and hallucinations of random glittering speckles lighting up my vision in a kaleidoscope of colors. Sometimes I'd hear fragments of conversations as though a ghost whispered in my ear. Occasionally, I'd black out and wake up somewhere unexpected. The worst part was the sensation that my body no longer belonged to me.

"Maybe we can prove efficacy." His lips curved into an I'm-gonna-win-the-science-fair grin.

"How? I don't have a pet monkey that we could keep up all night and then test cognitive function before and after dosing. And no way am I feeding KZ-9608 to my cat."

"We have something way better than an animal model. Nothing beats a human being with the actual condition."

"No way." I resisted the urge to throw his stupid bobble head at him.

"We've got the data from the safety and dose ranging studies in rats." He pointed to the notebooks. "So far there's no sign of toxicity from the parent drug or its metabolites."

"But we've never administered the drug to a creature bigger than your hand. You can't expect me to take an untested drug on a whim."

"I'll be the control subject." He stood up and bounced on his toes. "Our mini human trial is comparatively safer than you driving and running the risk of falling asleep at the wheel."

The idea of losing the chance to bring KZ-9608 to development made my heart hurt. My doctor had tried all of the FDA-approved treatment regimens, but none had stopped the symptoms.

I arranged the notebooks into numerical order and wiped a speck of dust off the self-defense certificate above my desk. Once, I was truly powerless, but since then I'd worked long and hard to regain control of my life.

"My dad's best friend is a bigwig at Kelvin Pharmaceuticals. Data from human subjects could be enough to convince him to sponsor the studies." With a tap, he set Elvira's head bobbing. "We doing this?"

I doubted pharmaceutical executives acquired drugs from graduate students dumb enough to test the compounds on themselves, but my desperation for a cure demanded I agree. "We can't take the drug simultaneously. One of us needs to record observations."

"Fine." He removed a quarter from his pocket. "Heads or tails?"

"Tails."

He flipped the coin, and George Washington's smug mug mocked me.

"I'll grab the doses." He shrugged into his lab coat and headed out the door.

The pit of my stomach ached in anticipation, stone-cold fear, or some toxic combination of both.

Minutes later, he returned with a small plastic bottle. "Two sprays per nostril should do the trick."

The knowledge that he'd prepared the dose before we'd agreed to take it whomped me like a kick to the kidney. We'd administered the drug orally and intravenously in the rodent studies, but never via the intranasal route.

If I wasn't desperate for a cure, I would have refused to spray that shit up my nose. Instead, I picked up the chilly-from-the-refrigerator bottle, and shot two sprays up each nostril. The mist smelled like a combination of spearmint and rubbing alcohol and it generated a burning sensation inside my nose. My eyelids seemed to be weighed down by barbells, and my vision faded into total darkness.

Liz's eyelids popped open and she surveyed her surroundings. Harmless-looking nerd in a white lab coat sitting at a desk, his attention focused on a plastic doll. Single escape route. Most accessible weapon—a pair of surgeon's scissors. Carbide cutting edges.

She wracked her brain for the reason she'd wound up in the unfamiliar office and came up empty. An old pro at dealing with a life consisting of patchwork pieces of stolen moments, she assessed the situation as safe.

Underneath the lab coat, the nerdy man sported jeans and a T-shirt featuring a voluptuous anime babe. Nervous energy seemed to come off him in waves.

The stink of his sweat and musky cologne evoked an urge to stab him with a pair of scissors. Then the scent of blood would overpower his offensive odor.

She took in the cheap white paint and the battered office furniture. At least she wasn't wearing a straitjacket or imprisoned in a mental institution. That's what happened to people like Liz. People with a hunger for violence and a craving for chaos.

"How do you feel?" The man's baritone voice belied his illusion of control. "Once you absorbed the drug, you passed out for a few minutes. Did you have an episode?"

"Lookie here, Geek Boy. If you had the nerve to slip me one of those date-rape drugs, I will end you." She yanked him close by the collar of his labcoat.

"Beth," he panted. "What's wrong? You took the drug of your own volition."

No way he possessed the balls or the stealthy skills needed to roofie her. Liz released him, headed over to the coffee pot in the corner, and poured herself a cup.

Drugs, other than caffeine, weren't her thing. She preferred being alert, ready to whoop ass before someone got the drop on her. It was her against the world. If she went down, she'd do it fighting.

Sitting in a submissive slouch, the guy rolled his chair closer to the door. She could easily reduce him to a bloody spot on the puke-green linoleum, but the sniveling sleaze wasn't worth the effort.

Liz gulped coffee and examined her outfit. Her scratchy white coat, high-waisted mom jeans, and an oversized polka-dot blouse wouldn't do. She tore open the coat, scattering pearly-white buttons, and undid all but two fasteners on her blouse, tying the tails into a knot to show off her cleavage and toned abs.

Better bait.

The geek gaped at her as though he expected a lap dance.

"Beth?" His words came out in a squeak. "I thought you hated coffee."

"Stop calling me Beth."

"What do you want me to call you?"

"An Uber."

"You can't leave." He stood with his arms crossed, and blocked the exit. Red splotches peppered his neck and cheeks. "I'm not done observing you."

She slammed down the cup, and coffee splattered the framed Krav Maga certificate on the wall above the other desk. "You've been watching me? Know what I do to perverts? I eliminate them."

"I-i-it's for the study. You can observe me next."

"And why would I want to watch you? Don't you think I can find someone better to look at?" She let out a sigh. "Give me your phone and wallet."

"This whole alpha female thing is sexy, but kinda scary." Hands shaking, he removed both items from his pockets and dropped them on his desk

She noticed his hands were shaking and viewed him in a new light. *Having a pet could be useful.*

A gangly, red-haired young man sporting a college logo sweat-shirt bounced into the office. He made a beeline for Liz and threw his arms around her neck.

"Beth." His breath was moist on her cheek. "Nice outfit."

Her heartbeat throbbed in her ears. She thrust the man away, grabbed the hole punch from the closest desk, and brought it down on Red's head. She delivered one powerful stroke for each word. "No. One. Touches. Me. Against. My. Will. Ever!"

She ended up on the dusty floor, straddling Red, her fingers clenched around the hole punch. Blood dripped from the metal onto the man's ruined flesh. Panting from exertion, she unflexed her fingers. The hole punch bounced off his body and fell to the tile floor with a clank.

Red's face was an abstract abomination of gore and gray matter. Other than her jagged exhalations, the only sound in the office was a keening wail.

The geek crouched in the corner, eyes wide.

The adrenaline faded, leaving Liz's muscles rag-doll limp and her brain buzzing. Her rage dissipated along with her patience. She wiped her hands on Red's sweatshirt and stalked over to the nerdy dude.

He cringed and brought his hands up. "B-B-Beth, please don't hurt me."

In order to strategize her next move, she needed quiet. She gave him a shake, yanked him to his feet, and kissed him breathless.

He tasted of cheese and bacon and wonder. His tongue invaded her mouth like a bloated earthworm. All of her energy shifted to fighting the urge to bite it off and shove the nasty thing down his throat. She pushed him away and swallowed the rest of her coffee to drown his foul taste.

The geek's gaze crawled over her body to rest on her chest. Normally, any kind of objectification would enrage her, but after the kiss his posture had changed. His shoulders were straight, and his chin held the cocky tilt of a man who expected to get laid rather than be slaughtered. Better to enlist his help in corpse disposal than to add another idiot to the body count.

"What's his deal?" She pointed to the dead guy.

"Roger was always kinda handsy." He shrugged. "Figured you would have filed a formal complaint if it bothered you."

Geek Boy clearly had her confused with someone else—someone weak. She nudged the body with her sneaker. "Actions speak louder than words."

"That they do. I'll tell the cops that Roger attacked and you defended yourself. Don't mention the drug. It's too soon to know if violent behavior is a side effect." He took a step backward. "Hey, don't look at me like you're going to lay a beat-down on me next."

"We can handle this ourselves by making Roger go bye-bye." She used a paper towel to wipe the blood splatter from her hands. "Surely there's somewhere we can stash him."

"The big walk-in freezer in the basement might work. Guess we can wrap him up with biohazard bags and wheel him on a cart."

"What are you waiting for?" She snapped her fingers.

"If I help you with this, you'll owe me. Are you okay with that kind of a debt, Beth?"

"The name's Liz." She grabbed his hand and squeezed. "I don't owe anyone anything."

A crease appeared above his forehead as though he worked multivariable calculus problems in his mind. "Alrighty. Be right back."

She cleaned up the blood on the floor, wiped down the hole punch, and forced herself to relax. Inside his desk drawer, she discovered a scalpel, which she wrapped in tissue and slipped into her sock. The nerdy guy wasn't the sharpest stiletto, but she doubted he was dumb enough to double-cross her. And if he did, she'd deal with his betrayal.

He returned with a wheeled cart and a bunch of large orange bags. Together they encased Roger's body in plastic and lifted him onto the cart. Miles pushed the cart down the hall, on to the elevator, and across the basement to the enormous walk-in freezer. All the while he muttered something unintelligible to himself.

The dimly lit basement stank of mold and rancid milk. With its dark corners and windy corridors, she thought the space could be the perfect setting for a slasher movie.

By the time they'd buried Roger in the back of the freezer behind a mountain of brown cardboard drums and returned to the office, Liz could barely keep her eyes open. She staggered and collapsed into an office chair.

"Subject walks, talks, and acts differently." The geek muttered to himself. "The half-life of KZ-9608 is shorter than expected, but I can work with that."

Liz was about to ask him what the hell he was talking about, but darkness overtook her.

I awoke disoriented, slumped in my office chair. My head throbbed with a monster hangover. No scientist worth her salt would agree to take an experimental drug that hadn't undergone rigorous safety testing. My despair over my disease had made me reckless.

Miles eyed me as though I'd grown a second head. "Beth?"

"I fell asleep. Guess the drug is a bust. Maybe it's me. There must be something about my body chemistry that renders narcolepsy drugs ineffective." A chill hit me, and goosebumps erupted on my skin. Holy hell, my blouse was half unbuttoned and tied to expose my midriff. A brown substance clung to my nailbeds, and my clothes were stiff with some kind of stain. A familiar dread crept down my spine. "What the hell did you do to me while I was passed out?"

"You wandered into the lab, got some of the rodent blood samples on your clothes, and started undressing." He shrugged. "Sleepwalking must be a side effect."

The idea of blacking out and doing things unconsciously in front of Miles made the hair on the back of my neck stand up. Slowly, I inhaled and let the air out, trying to calm my ragged breathing. Hyperventilating wouldn't help the situation. I'd sworn to never be powerless again, but this time my own mind was to blame—or rather, my brain on the drug I'd hoped would be my salvation.

"Let's dose you again so we can gather more data," he said.

"Hell no. I fell asleep. The compound must not work on me." I sniffed at one of the stains. "All I want to do is go home and take a shower. Dr. Rosenkrantz is going to lose his shit if we need to dose more rats to replace those lost blood samples."

"Come on. I tweaked the formulation and made a new batch of KZ-9608." He shook a white bottle in my face. "Let's give it a shot."

"If you want to take your turn as the guinea pig, be my guest. I'm done playing research subject." My skin itched. Letting the hot water wash away all the nastiness of the rat bloodbath sounded like heaven. "Either we do this right now or I'm heading home to shower. All this blood makes me feel like an extra in one of those slasher films you love so much."

"Okay. I'll dose myself and you can observe. I forgot to take your vital signs. Don't make the same mistake. The new formulation should work much better." He fumbled in his lab coat pocket, produced a bottle, and sprayed two quick bursts up each nostril. An X was scrawled on the bottom of the container in black marker. "Remember to take my vitals."

Twenty minutes or so later, he slumped forward in his seat.

I reached for his hand to take his pulse.

He lunged at me. Pinned me against the wall.

I tried to scream, but he covered my mouth with his hand.

Panic made me freeze. All of the self-defense classes I'd taken were useless. I shut down the same way I had when I was assaulted all those years ago.

He sprayed the drug up my nose and held me in place.

Tears streamed down my face, but I managed to bite his finger.

The backhand slap he delivered in return made my vison hazy. He held me in place for what seemed like hours, but was probably mere minutes.

I cursed him, cursed my disease, and cursed the emotions that likely triggered the muscle weakness that turned me into a floppy doll.

"You're going to pay for this." My slurred speech was likely indecipherable.

All of the hard work I'd done trying to mentally and physically rebuild after my attack didn't stop another man from taking advantage of me. The drug pulled me under its spell and the world fell away.

Liz came to with a jolt, fists clenched and ready to fight.

The geeky guy stopped spinning his shiny coin on the surface of the desk and crept over. "I made a fresh pot of coffee."

She relaxed, knowing she could control him with a punch or a kiss. "What? You want a medal or something?"

"No, but I have a proposal. This is gonna sound crazy, but hear me out. The drug appears to have a really unusual side effect." He handed a plastic rectangle to her. "This is your work identification card."

The woman in the photo wore a taupe turtleneck top and zero makeup—a look designed to blend into the background. Her poor posture screamed victim. The name on the card was Beth Howard.

"So what. Some chick with no fashion sense resembles me." She tossed the card at him.

It bounced off his chest and he flinched.

"That's you in the picture, but your current personality is only active while you're on the drug. Without it, you become Goody-goody Beth, and Luscious Liz ceases to exist."

As much as she longed to squeeze the life out of him, she couldn't kill him until she'd completely assessed the situation.

Her memories were full of holes. She remembered the rush of spotting men who looked willing and able to give her the rough romps she craved. She recalled lying in bed imagining beating an opponent with her fists or sliding a knife into flesh. Only sex and violence provided satisfaction.

She didn't hate men. They certainly had their uses, but nothing gave her a bigger thrill than delivering sweet retribution to those who tried to force themselves on her. One night a man had grabbed her ass in a bar. After coercing him outside and into an alley, she'd beat him bloody with a brick and stolen his wallet.

Her recollections weren't enough to piece together a whole life. The longest stretch she remembered was the time spent with Geek Boy and the red-haired guy she'd bludgeoned to death.

An existence made up of pieced-together bits didn't add up to a life worth living. She didn't want a sliver of the pie. She wanted the whole damned thing.

"When Beth discovers what you did to Roger, she'll do everything she can to suppress your personality. Once she has her way, you'll be gone forever."

Her stomach constricted.

"But I can stop Beth," he said. "Keep you alive and in control indefinitely. Do to her what she would have happily done to you." He stroked Liz's hair. "I synthesized a new, more potent batch of the drug. There's enough of the chemical to keep you in the driver's seat for a very long time. I'm exploring different delivery systems and formulations to decrease the dosing frequency. Each batch will be an improvement on the last."

"What's the catch?" In Liz's experience, any kindness required a sacrifice.

"I like you. Considering that kiss, you obviously like me."

She narrowed her eyes.

"Plus, I know where the body of the kid you killed is hidden."

"What keeps me from adding your corpse to the freezer?"

"Without my help, you'll be eradicated. If I didn't trick Beth and dose her, we wouldn't even be having this conversation." He grinned as though he'd been awarded the Nobel Prize. "If you want to live, you need to keep me happy."

"How did you trick this Beth?" The nerd didn't seem smart enough to fool another version of herself.

"I pretended to take the drug, but it was a placebo." He removed a plastic bottle from his coat and turned it sideways, revealing a mark scrawled on the bottom.

Liz leaned close to him.

He closed his eyes and tilted his head.

The idiot expected a kiss.

"Are you certain you're the one in control?" Her voice was as cold as the air in the deep freezer. She wrapped her arms around his neck and squeezed.

My eyes fluttered open. Miles's lab coat lay draped over the back of his office chair, but he was missing in action.

"Hey, asshole," I shouted.

Screw campus security. After I filed a police report, I'd contact the ethics committee. I never turned in the guy who beat me up and raped me. Regret over being too scared to report the crime had eaten away at my self esteem. This time I wouldn't let fear get in the way of justice. Miles would pay for what he'd done.

Pain radiated from my ankle and blood stained my pant leg. Carefully, I rolled up the denim and removed a tissue-wrapped metallic object from inside my sock. Before I could puzzle out why I had a scalpel in my sock, I noticed a cell phone on the corner of my desk. The scalpel slipped from my grip.

A green note was stuck to the phone screen. Someone had written the words "play the last video" on the paper. The handwriting reminded me of the messy scrawl I used while taking notes in class.

Cold fear crept up my spine. I imagined Miles making a recording of him taking advantage of me while I was unconscious, and I clenched my fists. My heart thumped.

I forced myself to breathe. To summon the courage to witness my shame. My hands shaking, I toggled to the correct screen and hit play.

The woman in the video resembled me. She even wore the same outfit. Yet, something was different. Something I couldn't pin down. I thought of how I could tell my identical twin cousins apart when even my aunt, their mother, continuously mixed them up.

"Geek Boy here made me an offer he thought I wouldn't refuse." The camera focused on Miles, who lay in a heap in the corner of the office. His arms and legs were bound with packing tape. A strip was wrapped around his head, sealing his mouth shut. He struggled and grunted. "But I'd rather come to an understanding with you than some random scumbag. I'm Liz, by the way." She waved.

A sense of déjà vu slammed me. I stopped the recording and replayed it from the start, examining every damning detail. The voice, the mannerisms, the clothing. I ran my fingers over the scar on my forehead from a middle-school skateboarding accident, half-expecting her to mirror me by stroking the identical mark on her face.

"Liz. Beth. Elizabeth." Each word tasted slightly different on my tongue.

The woman in the video was me but at the same time was a stranger. The hairs on my arms stood up like they did when I watched a horror movie about demonic possession. As a scientist, my lack of belief in possession didn't stop me from being scared.

"Geek Boy promised to use some drug he created to give me control of our body. To make you cease to exist. Said you'd do the same to me if you knew what I'd done. You might see things differently, but I protected us from that sleaze Roger. Trust me, the world's a better place without the likes of him."

I imagined the way the undergrad had found excuses to touch me, and my skin crawled. Once he'd made a game of trapping me in the giant basement freezer. While I'd screamed and screamed, the noise muffled by the thick walls and whirling fans, he'd laughed and laughed. Despite the chill, I'd broken into a sweat and my vision had gone blurry.

Eventually, he'd tired of the game and released me, but I hadn't stopped shaking for a long time afterward. I'd thought I'd never feel warm and safe again.

"Agree to my terms and you'll never see him or Geek Boy again. I'll handle everything." She tilted her head. "Double-cross me and I'll pin both their murders on you. If trusting you means the end of me, you're going down too."

I shivered. Getting shanked in the shower in prison was much more probable than getting stabbed by a motel psycho. Being incarcerated was to have every bit of control taken away indefinitely. I wouldn't last a week behind bars. If someone didn't kill me, I'd kill myself.

"You're a smart woman. A scientist, from the looks of things. If Geek Boy can make more of the drug that lets me come out to play, I'm certain you can, too. All I want is the chance to live. Let me run the show on the weekends, and you can have control during the week. In return, I'll clean up my mess and make all the bodies go bye-bye." She turned the camera back on Miles. "I know what you're thinking. Geek Boy doesn't look dead. Take a peek in your top desk drawer.

You'll find a little something of his in there. Ask yourself who deserves to live—both of us or a couple of Neanderthals who treat us as though we're some sort of sex doll created for their benefit. Give this a chance. Give me a chance. Give *us* a chance." The video ended.

I rolled the chair over to my desk, took a deep breath, and slid the drawer open.

Elvira's head lay on one side and the body of Miles's beloved bobble on the other. Gore covered both pieces. A twenty-five-cent piece was in between them. The rusted iron smell of blood mixed with the stench of fecal matter made me shudder. At least Liz had the common decency to line the drawer with paper towels, but I doubted that all the disinfectant in the universe could completely erase the disgusting odor.

I mulled over my options. Pretty much everything Liz said sounded crazy, yet it fit with Miles's actions. Maybe I had some form of dissociative personality disorder. Perhaps it was a side effect of KZ-9608, or maybe the drug simply triggered the switch in personalities. Liz could have been there all along. The theory explained my occasional blackouts, as well as the instances when I'd wake up and find myself in strange places.

I hadn't experienced sleep paralysis after being dosed with the drug, or hallucinations upon waking. Of the plethora of symptoms, the blackouts bothered me the most. If Liz's taking control of my body caused them, I could choose when they occurred by using the drug. It sure as hell beat being drugged out of existence or spending even a minute behind bars.

Liz offered me a get out of jail free card by promising to dispose of Miles and Roger's bodies, but I wasn't sure I should trust what amounted to my dark side.

Despite the heavenliness of the soft mattress, Liz valued her brief moments of life too much to linger in bed. The outfit of fitted jeans, gray T-shirt, and leather bracelet she wore was more her style than the mousey feminine fashion Beth preferred. A pair of boots with silver buckles sat at the foot of the bed with a green note stuck inside the right one. Inside the left one, she found a tissue-wrapped scalpel. She read the note and let out a whoop.

If you can't trust yourself, who can you trust? I'm in. —Beth

"Atta girl. A little trust is the first step to a successful partnership." Liz slid the boots on and wiggled her toes, enjoying the perfect fit. As she unwrapped the scalpel and turned it in her hand, sunlight glinted off the stainless steel. "After I get some coffee in me, it's time to play with my shiny new toy."

GUARDIAN OF THE FOUNDLINGS

by
Elsa M. Carruthers

Mikka sat at the bus stop, duffle bag in lap. Each time a truck came by, she hoped to see the blue line #22 right behind it. The bus was late, which meant that she'd get to the halfway house late too, and they might not even be open. A small lump formed in her chest. If the Faith Ways Home was closed, she'd have nowhere to stay for the night … a final "fuck you" from the California foster care system.

Dusk melted into night and at last the bus pulled over with a whoosh of exhaust. Mikka climbed on, handed the driver the voucher, and sat down in the back of the empty bus before she could get *the look* from the driver. She hated seeing those faces screwed up in a mixture of sympathy and pity when it was time to pay for something. Occasionally, a cashier wouldn't know what the paper voucher was for and Mikka would quietly explain, relieved to be doing something other than listening to the usual accompaniment of, "God will take care of you!" or "God bless you!"

After a winding ride through the outer city streets, the driver pulled over at a bent, rusted bus sign. She scurried off the bus, already noting that there were no lights on at the house across the street.

Please don't let it be abandoned.

The bus rolled away from the stop before she could tell him to please wait. The lump came back, and her eyes burned.

For fuck's sake.

No, she wouldn't cry; she just had to figure something out. No phone. She was never able to hide her small earnings long enough to afford one before Sylvie, one of the housemothers, stole them. A hot tear rolled down her cheek and she angrily swiped it away.

Sylvie would've probably stolen the phone anyway, so Mikka had to shrug it off. That was just one thing out of thousands of little things that robbed her and the other kids of their dignity, and she had no time for dwelling on it. She was at the edge of the little yard in less than a minute. This close, the house looked more tucked in for the night than abandoned.

Mikka decided to knock on the door anyway; no other ideas came to mind, and she didn't have enough money for a hotel, let alone know where there was one nearby. Her heart slammed in her chest as she climbed the steps to the door. Something was wrong. Faint voices came from inside, but other than that, the whole street was unnaturally quiet. She pulled the sheet of paper with the address out of her duffel.

Her half hope that she was at the wrong house died. The house numbers were there, just easily overlooked because they were painted on in a slightly darker muddy brown than the cracking plaster. A small, fading sign lay propped next to the door. Faith Ways Home. A big, squiggly-lined crucifix was painted below the letters in a garish mustard yellow that she assumed was meant to look like gold. But the place felt anything but holy.

Mikka rapped her knuckles on the peeling door. Two exposed, half-wrapped wires poked out of a hole where a doorbell was supposed to be. She waited. No one answered. The voices inside hushed.

Yeah, a nice welcome.

Mikka knocked on the door again. The talking stopped. Something thudded and a muffled call or laugh came from somewhere near the front door. It didn't quite sound right, though Mikka had heard a lot in her life that seemed off.

She waited, her breath caught in her lungs as if expelling it would somehow make the people go away. A moment passed, then another. She told herself that they just needed a bit of time to answer. Maybe they were tending to something and had to take care when going to the door.

She knew it wasn't true, but she had to quiet the growing alarm bells going off in her mind. After another minute or two passed, she knocked again. As she waited, she looked at the tall cinderblock wall that closed off the backyard. It was too tall to hop over.

This is bullshit.

Another knock; she had to. She took a deep breath before slamming the palm of her hand solidly against the door so that there could be no mistake that she was outside, trying to summon them.

The unmistakable sound of another door, probably a back door, slamming shut, and then silence.

She stood there, duffel bag starting to weigh on her left shoulder, feeling stupid. She also felt like she was being watched. There was a peephole in the door. Maybe she should stand directly in front of it. Mikka straightened up and knocked again. It was getting difficult to control her temper.

The sound of shuffling feet was unmistakable. Suppressing anger and panic, she tried friendly reason and spoke.

"Sorry I am late. I would've been here on time, but the bus was late and I … Maybe the home called you? Sylvie or Randy? The Faith Ways Home? My name is Mikka, and they should have told you I was coming." She couldn't shut up. "Please answer, they didn't give me enough money to go anywhere else and I am supposed to meet with my case manager tomorrow morning. Please."

A snicker.

"Assholes," she muttered. She couldn't let herself get mad; it would only get her in a ton of trouble. Mikka had seen what happens when you dish it out to these kinds of folks. They have it coming, but you were the one to wind up in jail or juvie.

She still felt terrible guilt at not being able to help Rick when he'd tried to protect his little brother from an undeserved beating. All she could do was try to distract Sylvie and Randy, but it hadn't work. They beat the poor little boy and got Rick arrested to boot.

Rumor was that he went to jail for assault, but no one had ever heard from him again. Worse, the little brother was sent to a different home and everyone lost track of him. Was it John, or Jim? She couldn't remember anything but his huge, scared eyes.

Mikka took a long breath. Then another. Her anger rose a notch, bordering on fury, but she felt a bit more in control of herself.

"Can I at least call my caseworker? Maybe she can find me somewhere else? I promise I will leave right after. I can even call from out here."

No answer for a while. And then a youngish sounding guy's voice shushing someone before saying, "Come back tomorrow. After ten."

"But I ..." Her appointment was at nine-fifteen, but it was useless talking to these people, even though she had to try. "My caseworker is expecting me. Carrie Walker at Child Services? Actually, if you could please just drop me off over there, I'll tell them how you helped me, and I'll never bother you again. They are supposed to reimburse you for gas, and they have a person on call twenty-four seven, so that won't be an issue..."

Wait. Are they even listening?

She didn't sense anyone on the other side of the door anymore. Did they just leave her to talk to the door?

Motherfuckers!

She had to go on. It was too cold to sleep outside.

Mikka stood still, straining to hear. Save for a slight scuttling that she couldn't pinpoint, there was silence. She raised her hand to knock again but stopped. What was the point? They'd ignore her and laugh anyway.

Tears ran down her face.

Who do these people think they are? Where do they think I'm going to go? Come back at ten? And then what? Fuck!

It was obvious they didn't care. Didn't care that she had nothing and no one. Didn't care that she had nowhere to go and no way to support herself, didn't care that she'd lived a mostly miserable, invisible, survival-centered existence. They gave no fucks.

And wasn't that the sum of her whole life? Just a series of run-ins with people who gave no fucks? She slinked back down the steps and sat. The depth of her situation, and all she'd been through up until now, hit her at once. Uncontrollable sobs poured out of her and shook her body. Normally she'd never give anyone the satisfaction of watching her break down, but she was just too tired and angry to fight anymore. She'd definitely fix them if she ever got the chance.

She kept on sobbing until she was spent. The temperature dropped as the rain suddenly became a heavy downpour. She crept back onto the stoop, settled in against the door as discreetly as possible and fell half-asleep.

Just as she was drifting into a dreamless sleep, her jaw clenched tight with pent-up fury, the door suddenly pulled open. A smelly, wadded-up blanket was unceremoniously dumped on her. Mikka sat up immediately. She had never been more insulted. Before the asshole could shut the door, she pushed her duffel in the way and jumped to her feet.

The guy, not much older than her, took a startled step back and she pushed the door open. It slammed shut behind her. His mouth went slack as he stared at her. He shifted his gaze to the shut door and then back at her.

The house was grimy with layers of greasy filth along the doorways. From her position in the front room she could see a hallway to the right, an eat-in kitchen adjoining the room she was in, and, to the left, a narrow staircase that must lead to the one or two bedrooms on the top floor.

It was a typical, squeezed-up row house. The linoleum floor in the kitchen curled and bubbled in places and seemed somehow obscene. The filthy shabbiness of this place—this was supposed to be her last stop before she was emancipated by the state? It had the unmistakable feel of a bachelor/party pad. Weren't there inspections? Mikka's outrage got the best of her.

"Just what the fuck did you think you were doing, throwing that nasty blanket at me?"

The guy stepped back and gave her a stupid simpering look, as if she was being unreasonably demanding. His lips opened and closed, then he finally croaked, "Thought you might be cold."

Does he even hear himself? Does he think I'm that stupid? No.

No, she'd enough.

Mikka snapped.

"Like I'm a fucking dog? The door's not broken. You couldn't let me in like any decent person would do? You're getting paid for me to stay here, right?"

Before he could open his stupid mouth to answer, Mikka's voice rose to a scream. "And I bet it is a shit-ton more than they give me in vouchers!"

He backed into the wall and she followed, still screaming. "Where was the other guy? Is he in the back, or upstairs?"

He didn't say anything, and that sent Mikka over the edge again. Before she could think about it, she shoved a cheap coffee table over, breaking off one of the legs. She kicked the overturned table, and the broken corner splintered.

The guy cowered.

Not sated, Mikka grabbed the leg and clubbed him with it. A curl of satisfaction rose inside her. She hit him again.

The guy's cellphone fell to the floor. He was probably trying to call the police or nine-one-one, and she was having none of that. Mikka stomped on it and then flung it so hard against the wall that the screen shattered, and the phone's inner components scattered.

She whacked him with the table leg again. One of her blows landed flat on the side of his head and ear and he wailed. She hit him so many times she broke the leg across his face. Blood oozed around his head, and the scent of iron filled the air. A sickening crunch came from his nose and he feebly pushed at her hand before going still.

A feeling of being watched made her turn. She sensed someone in the shadows, though she couldn't quite be sure.

There might be just this guy ...

A small, metallic clink sounded from the kitchen and she very slowly and carefully walked into the room. A smaller guy about the same age as the other, but already sporting a soft middle and a receding hairline, crouched by a late-model fridge. In his hand he had a large kitchen knife. Mikka was sure that it came from a knife block somewhere. That was the sound she'd heard.

Coward let his friend get killed and came in here to save himself.

"I called nine-one-one. They are on their way," he said in a very surprising baritone voice.

Mikka doubted that. These kind of people never called the police—not if they could help it. In fact, she was almost positive of that, and if she had to guess, they had all kinds of things they worked hard at hiding.

Just in case, she rushed at him and stopped in front of him, breathing hard. He flinched and she laughed at him. "Good!" she screamed at him.

His gray eyes flickered and shifted away from hers.

"What?" he seemed very confused.

Uh-huh.

"I was supposed to be here. Somewhere there's paperwork. When the police get here, I'll tell how you two tried to hurt me."

"What?" he asked again. "No, that's not what happened," but she could tell that even as he said it, he heard how idiotic he sounded. His knife lowered a tiny bit.

"Really? That's what you're going to tell the cops? How are you going to explain the knife you're holding when they get here?"

Then he smiled. It was ugly. He lifted the knife up again and stood straighter. "No one is coming."

He lunged at her. She fell under his weight and he laughed as he pushed the tip of the blade into the top of her breast before pulling it out.

"Aw, you're so small," he mocked her. "Jamie should've been able to take you out."

Mikka said nothing. She was caught under him and he leaned into her in such a way that she couldn't take a deep breath. He made a half dozen other short stabs into her chest and shoulders.

The more she squirmed to get out from under him, the more he cut off her air. Her vision went gray and she felt herself start to slip under a heavy cloud of exhaustion. Part of Mikka's brain told her to fight harder, to get up, or he'd kill her. The other part of her brain couldn't listen.

I must be going into shock.

For some reason, that thought wasn't enough to fully rouse her.

Mikka sputtered. Something wet, hot and salty ran into her mouth and her wounds burned. With a huge effort she opened her eyes to see him standing over her, zipping up his fly.

He bent to slap her in the face. "You need to clean up after yourself in the front room. And take care of Jamie. You can't just leave him out there."

"Did you just piss all over me?" She couldn't believe it.

"Yeah, you stupid cunt. You can't come in here and kill my friend."

He was fucking crazy and he still had that damned knife in his hand.

She was about to say so, when he stood and kicked her so hard, she both felt and heard her lower ribs snap. It took a second to catch her breath. The pain was like nothing she'd ever felt; the only thing worse was the time Sylvie touched the tip of her iron to Mikka's forearm.

"Get up!" he screamed.

She got to her feet as he stood back, watching her. Just as Mikka was standing, he kicked her leg and she fell to the floor. She was bleeding hard from at least seven places and her side pinched and seared. When he laughed and spit on her, the humiliation and helplessness washed over her. All the years of abuse and rejection …

Fuck this!

Mikka took a ragged breath and stepped right into his face. He tried to jerk away. She smiled at him and she saw the fear in his eyes. When he raised the knife above his shoulder to strike her, she punched him in his soft gut at the same time.

"Ooomph," he gasped and dropped the knife. She squatted down to fetch it, her broken rib stabbing her insides as she twisted. God, it was terrible.

She grabbed the blade of the knife first because it was nearest her and she didn't dare take her eyes off him. It bit deep into her palm. Switching her grip to the handle, she stabbed upward from where she crouched. The knife went to the hilt in his right leg. With effort she pulled it out and stabbed him again and again, even stepping on his feet and climbing atop his falling form for purchase.

All the while he was slapping and punching her, and she was numb to it all. She heard his cries and screams as though from a long distance. When she finally stopped to stretch her back, she saw the blood. It pooled around him.

Something possessed her to dip her fingers in it and smear it under her eyes in two bold swipes. She screamed in triumph.

"Fuck you! Fuck you! Fuck you!"

Knife still in hand, she limped back to the first guy to make sure he was dead. Mikka scrambled up the stairs once she was sure neither would ever get back up. Both rooms smelled of mold and dirty, mildewed clothes and rotting food. She riffled through drawers until she found what she knew she would.

Her hands trembled. Mikka knew she would see things that belonged to other foster kids and small clothes, but … It was the boy's Spiderman action-figure. She knew it was his because it was chewed on the corner, and god, she just put it all together.

The boy, John, that was his name, she remembered Randy yelling at him to throw the toy out. He was sent here first, and when they got tired of him or it looked too suspicious to keep him longer, they sent him off to some other shithole.

In the closet of the second room lay a stash of things stolen from other kids like her. There were earrings, necklaces, vintage pocket watches, pouches with tiny things, pearl-handled pocket knives, lockets and other items precious only to those that carried them. Atop it all was an antler rack.

Without thinking, she placed it on her head. It fit snugly. Then she gathered the things. She put what she could in her duffle to give them back. The thought filled her with a wonderful sense of purpose.

But first, she had things and people to take care of. She went to the bathroom in search of medical tape for her ribs. Mikka knew not to wrap them, but she needed stability until she could better take care of herself.

It was only an hour or so until daybreak and she was excited to begin. A spontaneous smile spread across her face. The rack on her head fit like a crown. Her mascara streaked down to the stripes of blood on her face and she never felt more beautiful. Rescuing the kids at Lourdes Home was going to be fantastic.

"Protector," she said aloud. Then, "No, Guardian. Guardian." Mikka liked that a lot. She would protect and guard them until they could fend for themselves. She'd show them how.

She remembered that one of the houses on the street looked like a good place to stay. The others looked burned out. Squat pads that Mikka knew to stay well away from. But the one on the end was likely abandoned. Hopefully clean. Maybe owned by an absentee landlord. It would do nicely for her.

The duffel, filled with much of the stolen goods, banged heavily as she dragged it downstairs. She had to leave some of the items because her bag was full to almost bursting. When she went through the dead men's pockets for cash, she found a roll of twenties on each. A couple hundred at least. She'd have to come back for the rest of the items, but for the moment, she'd return what she could.

Without looking back, she left the two assholes to rot.

Mikka made plans as she walked. There was a lot to do and for the first time she could remember, she felt good.

MOTHER OF ALL

by
Leadie Jo Flowers

The tree's girth spread at least two hundred years wide as the saws shrieked the blood-curdling scream of death for the ancient one. They cut the wedge out of the tree so it would fall in the direction causing the least damage to the wood. The tree wobbled, but it didn't fall.

"What the hell?" Boss Man mumbled while scratching at his cheek. He looked up at the leaves blowing in the direction they anticipated the tree to fall.

Hidden from him, Oddudua held on tight to the tree, waiting for the right moment.

"Keep a lookout," Diego called as he ran to the opposite side of the cut in the tree. "I'll give it a tip."

He shoved with his massive weight, but the tree stood solid.

"Maybe we need to cut her further back?" Sebastian said.

Boss Man shook his head. "I never seen anything like this. Is there a limb caught on something round back?"

"No, but it looks like there might be something or someone way up top. I can't make it out," Sebastian called.

Boss Man and Diego ran around the back. But the shape circled to the other side. They ran to the front again, stepping farther back to see what it was. The branches and leaves blocked most of the view.

"Sebastian, head out that way and see if you can figure out what's going on." Boss Man pointed towards the landing point, an area no tree cutter wanted to venture into.

About forty yards out, Sebastian cupped his mouth. "It looks like a damned person! Get over here!"

The guys had run nearly halfway there when they heard the crack. The tree fell with lightning speed. Diego and Boss Man never stood a chance. Diego had his massive lower body pounded into the ground.

Boss Man's chest was deflated by a thick branch while one running off it cracked his head open like an egg. Sebastian, farthest out, lay impaled to the ground by a branch through his gut.

Silence claimed the forest. Sebastian knew he wouldn't make it through the day. The tree shifted and he heard a scream, unaware it was his own before all turned black.

A hand brushed his cheek as he blinked, turning from the sun to see a woman sitting near him.

"Do you want me to help you die?"

"Who are you?" Sebastian choked out through his dry lips, tears washing the dust from the sides of his face.

"Oddudua. I go by many names. You shouldn't take what isn't yours."

He looked at her sitting naked and calm. Perhaps a ghost come to claim his soul. He laughed but the searing pain cut him off. "You did this. You pushed the tree on us, didn't you?"

"Yes, you come here and destroy everything, so I stopped you. I am the protector of this place and mother to all nature. But I have a heart for suffering creatures like you. I can let you die slowly by yourself, or I can make it quick."

He groaned as the tree moved ripping at his insides a bit more. "Please … make it quick."

She slid her hands on each side of his head and started applying pressure. He looked into her eyes and she let him see in her world. She felt his pain and understanding as his lips moved.

"No, no…" The cracking of his skull resounded like the tree's scream before it fell.

Oddudua stroked the fallen tree tenderly.

She sat near the river, her tears flowing into the water. "My children, I don't know how to save all of you. What must I sacrifice?" A doe nudged her arm, forcing her to look up, to look out over the land and into her fawn's innocent eyes. They both answered her.

Others followed with their answers. The plants, animals, and Earth itself talked to her. They sang their sorrows and losses. Their energy took her to the places where she was needed most. The fires, not natural fires but the ones set to clear the land. The farmers burned everything, so she helped those who started them. She stood in the flames, beckoning them to her open arms. She called them by name, and they ran to her, to her nakedness, perhaps to save her as the flames licked her body. She embraced them as the flames melted and bubbled their bodies, muffling their screams in her breasts.

Hundreds of thousands of years ago when fires raced through the lands she would run to the people to save them, shelter them and chase death away. Now, she laid their crisped bodies in the ashes before she brought the rain to douse the flames and grow the seeds. Their bodies would not be a waste, as they nourished the new seedlings.

The farmers stopped coming so often. Some desperate young farmers braved the stories of these men's burning deaths, trying to move on to other forests to destroy. When the wives followed their husbands to make sure they stayed safe, Oddudua reached out to them. Slipping into their minds, she sang in her hypnotic voice, a voice only they could hear above their husbands' screams.

She didn't want to leave their children orphans. She kept the wives trapped in her song until their husbands' cold hearts had stilled. Then she sat and cried with her daughters.

As the winds changed, she followed them to a northern forest where her children called to her. She winced at their sudden pain as their beating hearts stilled. Their numbers were many. Nearly to the gun carrier she cringed at the sound of the blast echoing past her. The deer lay bleeding, but not fatally. Oddudua appeared in the gunner's sights. He lowered his weapon from his face, blinked a couple of times, and then ran towards the animal.

Having seen these weapons operate many times over, she wrapped her hand over his on the gun butt. Grabbing the opposite end of the rifle, she twisted it back towards his head, sliding the muzzle under his chin. The recoil of the gun caught her off guard, but not so much as the spray of blood and brain matter across the forest floor. Momentarily she felt the loss of her human child—like the others, humans too were hers. But the loss of many outweighed the loss of one.

There were others. She could smell them. She approached the hunters one by one to assist them in meeting their doom, until she met the fourth. His eyes were those of a young man, really, still a boy. A tear fell from her eye as she walked up to him and stroked his face as lightly as a feather. His mouth dropped open, mimicking a silent scream as she tried to calm him. Gently taking the gun from him, Oddudua saw his face, a younger, thinner face of the first man whose life she had taken, maybe his father or another relative.

Feeling his pain and confusion, she spoke: "It is not right to kill. Yes, some animals kill each other for food. But your people, your race, takes and tortures those which you don't need. You kill the imperfect for the sake of paper, you call it money, it's paper from trees killed, paper that makes you think you are valued. You put beautiful animals' heads on walls to make yourself feel powerful. It isn't necessary. I'm sorry for your loss."

The boy took off running. Running to the man she now heard him call Dad. She tried to stop the pain as she heard his screams. Hopefully the young man would never touch a gun again.

On the frozen tundra, she watched as a group of sealers grasped their hakapiks by the long wooden handle, swinging them to check the balance with the large metal hook. While they couldn't hurt her, she didn't want to chance them getting away and telling people about her as the hunter boy from the forest had done. For her it didn't matter, but the young man's life was destroyed.

They eventually decided he was seeing things—it was just the shock of finding his father's body. But it didn't explain the three other hunters' bodies. Four suicides in the same group? The only thing that saved him was his small size; they couldn't fathom him being able to successfully take on all four of them.

Oddudua had felt what the boy had gone through, the hell of being accused of killing them all, including his father. Now she cloaked herself in white, nearly invisible on the tundra. Still too close to each other for her to get them all. She had to wait for them to separate.

The more the sealers distanced themselves from each other the easier it would be for her to take each one without raising suspicion. She went to the farthest one. It was quick, and he had no chance to reflect on what happened. Keeping herself between the others and him, she grabbed the hakapik, spun it around and, with a slight crunch, buried it in the base of his skull. Moving to the next sealer, she used the same tactic. She had to work quickly as the boat was waiting for the men to bring their hauls back.

She heard the boatmen talking over the silence of the ice, the occasional soft splash as a seal slipped into the water.

The lookout searched the horizon for the sealers. None were visible. He picked up his binoculars and scanned the horizon again.

He cupped his mouth towards the bridge. "Captain, no visual on the hunters."

The captain came down and picked up the binoculars. He made a whistling sound, sucking air in between his teeth. "Grab a couple men and take the guns with you. Just check to be sure there aren't any people out there trying to stop us. Oh, and take a flare gun."

The lookout found the first body and fired the flare. He reloaded and let out a yelp just before Oddudua buried the hakapik in him. She hadn't been fast enough; more would come.

The boatmen came in groups of two or three. Usually she could get between them in her white cover and finish them off before the other would have a chance to understand what had happened, then the other would go down and then the third. She was getting faster at this. After a hunt the ice usually ran red from the sealers' butchering, but now there were only thin streams of blood from hakapik wounds. The hunters would lie frozen until found.

She found the captain on the bridge waiting for a report. "Why do you kill these animals?" she said.

The captain jumped at her voice. "Who the hell are you?" He looked around for the other men.

"They won't be coming back." The hakapik buried in his head before he could respond.

When all was said and done, the dead lay still and quiet.

Oddudua moved on towards the discord of cries. She found her human children, so thin, their eyes bulged as loose skin hung from their cheekbones, their stomachs bloated. Mothers cradled their children with no tears left to weep, knowing they were losing their children. She searched for the cause, for the reason they had no food. The buildings lay in pieces, hollowed by bombs, but she saw no soldiers. Only the dying. She tried to ease the pain of the mothers and help the children's souls move on. She sat in a lone tree, waiting, thinking.

The dull drone of approaching planes caught her attention, though she thought nothing of it until she saw the people running and the bombs falling. *Are these the soldiers who did this?* She heard shots ringing out and tried using the winds to force the whistling bombs to less populated areas, but she couldn't stop the bullets. She stooped inside a cockpit behind the pilot. She twisted his head with a jerk before he ever saw her. She steered the plane to a field and let it crash, moving on to the next.

The next time she wasn't so fortunate, as the pilot grabbed for a gun hidden in his jacket. She watched his finger flip the auto-pilot on.

Half-turned around, he asked, "How did you get in here?"

She heard quivering in his voice. She said, "Why do you kill these people?"

"Answer my question!" His hand was shaking as he kept glancing out the window.

"I go where I want, when I want. I can do that. Can you?"

"Put your hands up!"

She raised them so her elbows were level with her shoulders, her hands resting on the ceiling. She smiled, "What will that accomplish? Why are you killing these people?"

"I have orders to bomb this place. There are terrorists there."

"No, there are women, mothers and their babies. Few men are left. You might look elsewhere for them."

"No, not possible. I have orders and this is the place, they're hiding here. Sit down, put your hands on your head and cross your legs."

She did, but soon the guns rattled on. She clenched her fists. Then, reaching around him, she grabbed the control wheel. She forced the plane straight towards the ground.

"No! What are you doing? My family, children, what—"

A fiery ball rose from the twisted metal and the silenced man. He had a family, children, but he was killing. *Why?* He was her child as much as everyone else on the planet. Pacing back and forth as the others called to her, she understood another choice was necessary. *Who do I deal with first? Which cries require my help most?*

Oddudua dove deep in the oceans to find the nets being dragged across the floor of the ocean, ripping up everything in their way. When she slashed them open the fish escaped and the plants fell listlessly back to the bottom. By the time she reached the boat the fishermen were throwing in new nets.

"Why are you killing everything?" Her voice carried across the boat and out over the ocean. The men looked around for the source.

The captain pushed a switch. "Is the PA system on?"

The operator's voice drifted back. "No, I heard it down here as well. I already radioed out for other ships in a ten-mile radius from our position to check in with us. No response yet."

Standing next to the captain she whispered in his ear, "Catching fish is one thing, destroying the environment while doing so is pure greed."

He spun around looking for her.

She made herself visible while dodging his arm. "It's not nice to hit people."

"What do you want? Who are you? Get off my ship!" He swung at the air, hoping to connect with her.

Oddudua increased the speed of the winds. The waves rose higher and higher, breaking over the side of the ship, pushing it and rolling until it finally flipped upside down, throwing the fishermen overboard. The men inside the ship struggled to escape but most of them drowned. The couple who made it to the top struggled to exhaustion before succumbing to the ocean.

She found rivers and streams discolored and choked with chemicals and dead fish. She blocked pipes and jammed machinery, but the mechanics only unclogged the pipes and repaired the machines. She dammed up the rivers flowing with plastic waste only to have the dams broken. By the time Oddudua finished with one, the previous was operational again.

How could I stop all this?

If she didn't kill, they continued to kill. Her rage grew stronger as each day passed. There were so many of them and only one of her. Even with her powers it was becoming impossible to keep up. She called out to the other gods even though they had disappeared hundreds of years ago. As always, their silence rang in her ears as the suffering cries deafened her.

There had to be other ways to stop them, to stop this disaster, this killing of Earth. She watched and listened, learning more and more. As she did, she understood that most of the people only did what they were told to survive. It was higher, more important people telling them what to do who were the problem.

She eliminated a few of them. It was easy. She helped them slip off a bridge, she caused car crashes, and even arranged accidents where they worked, but it seemed like someone was always waiting to take their place the next day. She needed to understand why these people were given these orders, where were they coming from.

Again, she listened and followed the path, higher and higher. There were groups of people who started the process, rich, powerful, and with no conscience. She created more accidents with them, like the fire that killed off most in one case, but they too were quickly replaced.

She realized that the entire system they were under was broken, that people no longer cared. Of course, she found some who did, but how could she save them without eliminating the others?

Learning more, she followed the path of orders, hovering near offices and boardrooms. It became clearer how many people were just followers of the few. The means of their survival depended on following orders.

Copying their actions, she practiced their walk, look, and voices while trying to save some of her children at the same time. Feelings of dread and guilt filled her being. When she let people see her, they treated her like the others. But killing her children who were killing her other children was a vicious cycle with no end. *Is there no way to win this?*

If there was even a small chance, she had to try.

She walked into a major corporate office, her head held high, balancing in the worthless shoes that had to be torture devices. It only added to her frustration. She approached the receptionist. "I need to speak with the CEO."

"I'm sorry but he isn't available." The receptionist looked down at her desk and began writing.

"Excuse me, I'm a shareholder of this company and I need to speak with the CEO, urgently." Oddudua managed to keep her voice at an acceptable level.

"What is the nature of your business?" The woman smiled, her pen poised to write.

"Do you want the long version or the short one?" Oddudua noticed the guard turn towards her. She took a deep breath. "I'm here about the problems all over the news about the pollution. I'm here to help."

The secretary moved the pen but wrote nothing. Oddudua searched the young woman's mind. She was her child as well, but she wanted to teach her about respect, about sympathy and empathy, that she was not the only one of importance. The "child" enjoyed the power of controlling people and wanted more of it.

"Who are you with?" the receptionist snapped at Oddudua.

"What do you mean?" Oddudua wasn't sure this was the right question. The receptionist refused to give any direct answers to her; her statements avoided dealing with her. She would be quite happy if Oddudua walked out, but she wasn't finished with her, yet.

"What organization sent you here?" The receptionist's voice was sharp as a knife. Her expertise at dancing around questions qualified her as a politician, giving no real answers, if any at all.

"I represent myself, no others." All the lifeforms of the world reminded Oddudua why she was here. "Unless you want to count life itself."

The receptionist smiled up at her as she reached under her desk. "I understand. I will see what can be arranged."

"I'm trying to be polite here. It's quite simple. When can I have an appointment to speak with him?"

"As I said before, I'm afraid that's not possible right now. He isn't available." Looking Oddudua in the eyes, she finished: "Ever."

Oddudua felt rather than saw the door open behind her but stayed calm. "I really need time to speak with—" Someone grabbed her arm from behind.

"Come with us." Two security people stood beside her. One held her arm in a firm grip.

Oddudua resisted sending their bodies flying halfway around the world. "I just want to make an appointment. Is this not allowed?"

"Madam, let's go." He gave a gentle tug. She knew she shouldn't do it. But without any concern for the consequences, she waved her arm in a smooth motion, sending them both across the room into the wall. She smiled, turning to the receptionist with a look as fake as the receptionist's.

"Is it not permitted to make an appointment to speak with someone here?" She stared at the receptionist as she held her hand up behind her. The guards struggled to get up but couldn't.

The receptionist stared in fear at the guards. "May I have your n-name please?"

"Let's go with the formal name. Oddudua. Now, may I have an appointment?"

Still staring at the struggling guards, the receptionist began to write. "I will need your last name and phone number please."

"Just a day and time will be fine. I will be here at the appointed time."

"But I don't know when he will be available. Please, may I have a phone number?"

Oddudua noticed the young woman's hand beginning to tremble ever so slightly. She reached across the desk with her free hand and touched her shoulder. The trembling stopped and the woman relaxed a bit in the chair. She was strong, but still afraid.

Oddudua smiled. "Which office is he in?"

The receptionist resisted answering and Oddudua pushed her mind a bit more.

"I'm sorry, I didn't hear what you said."

The receptionist's mouth moved before she uttered, "Top floor."

Oddudua found his office empty.

She chose this company for the conservatory balcony in the boardroom. She felt more at home there and could blend in with the plants until she was ready to make herself known. Making herself comfortable, she listened to their droning on and on about bullshit. It was a new word she liked, and so appropriate! Using the surrounding magnetism, she concentrated it to seal off the room and all their electronic devices before revealing herself.

"Who are you?" the middle-aged man at the opposite end of the table nearly shouted. "How did you get in here?"

Oddudua calmly circled the table. "That is not important. What is important is how you see your company and where you see it going. Right now, it's not going to last very long if you keep destroying everything around you."

"What the hell are you talking about?" The CEO coughed at the opposite end of the table as his pudgy finger pushed the button to the secretary. "Get security up here now and call the police." His voice was shaking almost as much as the huge jowl that bubbled out of his tied-off neck.

"She can't hear you. No one can. I tried to make an appointment, but they wouldn't let me talk to you. So," she walked around the table looking at each person and smiling at them, "I decided to talk to you on my terms."

"Who are you?" said an immaculately dressed and coiffed woman, repeating the obvious question of the day.

"Oddudua, or Mother Nature. I am the guardian of all life, even yours. But I have run into a problem. So many of you humans are killing off each other as well as all other forms of life that are keeping you alive. I tried to stop the ones who were directly killing the trees, fish, animals, everything that is living. In doing so I was killing people. But you are my children just as much as everything else living. What am I to do now? I don't want to kill my children who are killing my other children for profit. So, what are we going to do about this?"

All sat in silence waiting for the other to speak until Mr. Jowls coughed again.

A middle-aged man, who spent a good deal of time in the gym, stood up. "We are an entity who has to answer to our shareholders. They want dividends, growth, not to save the planet!" He slammed his hand down on the last word.

Oddudua rolled her eyes, speaking calmly. "There is something you fail to see. Without this planet, these other lifeforms, including yourself, you will cease to exist." She took a deep breath. "Do you understand this? Cease to exist, as in dead! Does that mean anything to you?"

The coiffed woman held her head high, perhaps to pull the wrinkles out of her neck. "We will fix those problems in time. For now, we must grow the company. Would you have any specific suggestions to make?"

"Yes, clean up your act. Stop polluting. Find other ways to do what you do."

A young wall of a man looking like a bouncer jumped up and tried to grab her. He was nowhere near grabbing her and hit the floor. She smiled as he looked up at her.

She waved her finger at him. "It's not nice to fool around with me, young man!" With a flip of her hand she sent him flying into the wall with a solid smack.

The secretary dropped her pad and ran for the door, yanking and twisting the knob, but the door remained tightly closed.

"Do you understand that I can kill all of you," Oddudua said while walking in circles around the table, "then walk out of here, and nothing will happen to me?"

An older man spoke, barely audible. "You would be caught eventually. Whatever group you represent doesn't matter, but we will listen to you. Present your complaints and we will discuss them."

"The only group I represent is the living on this planet, including yourself. I represent you. I am trying to show you the errors of your ways, to help you, to make things better so this planet survives with you on it. The alternative is that Earth survives without you, because the human race is no longer part of the food chain. Do I make myself very clear?"

"What are your demands?" he asked with a louder tone.

"Simple, stop polluting. Stop destroying nature with all the resources you are using. Find a better way to run your business without destroying everything you touch. Instead of coal and gas, use the wind, sun, or other types of energy. It really isn't complicated."

"Do you know how much that would cost us? The shareholders would kick us all out on the street," the bubbling jowl growled as his face burned bright red.

She could sense he was near his demise. As she walked by him, she rested her hand on his shoulder. His health was very poor. She wasn't sure which health issue was going to kill him first. It wouldn't take much from her to help him on his way. She just wasn't ready. They needed a chance to show her they could change. And it was now or never. They needed a solid plan. And it needed to be enforced.

"Here is what we are going to do," she said. "You are going to create a plan now on how you will run this company and what you will do to meet my demands. If you don't, I will take each and every one of your lives. This is not a game. You will change your ways, or no one lives, at least no humans." She smiled.

"But our competitors will run us into the ground. We will be bankrupt in a year." It was the young man who had slid across the floor.

The woman at the door finally let the handle go and took her seat.

Oddudua listened to them argue and complain about the same thing repeatedly. When they were hungry, she provided them with her bounty, to which the dying jowls at the end of the table complained. Time passed in a way they could not comprehend. She finally agreed to some of their plans and demanded a strict deadline on everything.

Mr. Jowls raised his voice for the umpteenth time. "It will take time. Let us out of here so we can get started. Factory changes can take two or more years. Be patient with us."

She gave them her motherly smile. "I know you are all tired. You have done well. But none of you is sincere in following through with these plans. Not one single person in this room. This is what I am going to do. For every deadline you miss, one of you will die. And your competitors will do and suffer the same, because they are on the line. Just like you, they too will die. Do I make myself very clear?"

They all nodded even though it was only an act. As with the others, she was going to have to make an example out of one of them. And if they all didn't work together, it would be the end of humanity.

"None of you is believing any of this." They gave her a blank stare, exhausted. "Here is what I'm going to do. If you and all your companies do not comply with our agreements, not only will you die, your families and friends will as well. Because I will create so many natural disasters aimed at humanity that you will be nearly, perhaps completely, wiped out. As for now, I will make an example of one of you."

Mr. Jowls's eyes glazed over as he sat motionless for a moment before slumping over on the table. Oddudua experienced a deep disappointment. This was too easy; the man was already nearly dead.

"Leave him alone." She waved at the two board members who rose to assist him. "He would have been dead in a matter of days. Not really a fair warning, so I'm going to take another one."

"But you said you would only take—" The coiffed woman gagged, gurgling as plants from the seeds in the fruit she had eaten earlier began to bloom from her mouth, nose, and ears. Her lips turned blue, tears rolled down her face, and then her face shaded blue, not a pretty color on her, before collapsing.

She waited, and some deadlines were met and others weren't. They fought with her, but they always lost in the end. The sharehold ers did go against them and some were kicked out. It really wasn't their fault, but she held to her promise. So, they died, and she went for the shareholders next.

Since the shareholders were so many, Oddudua decided to let nature do her work, with a little controlled help from her. The Pacific tectonic plate suddenly slipped under North America. The tsunami was grand as it wiped out the entire West Coast thirty or more miles inland. Cities were gone. A bonus she didn't expect was the eruption of Yellowstonc's volcano from the pressure of the shifting plate. Oddudua warned the others of her actions, but they didn't believe she caused it.

It was like a chain reaction after that. Billions of people became millions. Entire infrastructures were wiped out. Then the millions became thousands as the longest winter since the previous ice age set in.

Oddudua decided she would see if the survivors would change the world. They had to start over again but she had already decided that the greedy, power-hungry people would meet an early demise. Even if it meant killing off the very last of mankind.

We Are the Weirdos

by
Kerri-Leigh Grady

Mackenzie's breath hitched when Mr. Franco walked Jake to the front office door, his hand resting on the football player's shoulder, chuckling at something Jake said. He might as well have waved the fucker a fond farewell, a happy toodaloo to send the guy on his way back to class. Why had she bothered reporting Jake? She'd been naïve to think he would see any consequences. Not in this school. Not in this town. Probably not even in this country.

While Mr. Franco was the principal, boys would get away with anything.

She willed her face to relax. If Franco thought she wasn't calm, he'd win. He seemed to enjoy it when his decisions upset students.

When Franco turned to her, his perpetual sneer was in full force, and the cloud of slick brown she normally sensed around him was spiked with bile yellow. "In my office, young lady."

She followed him inside and waited for the invitation to sit, but he never offered. Instead, he sat behind the heavy wooden desk and glowered at her, his lips pursed and his chin resting on steepled fingers like a pretentious asshole. Appropriate.

He finally crossed his arms and sat back in his chair. The leather seat creaked in response. "You claim he made contact without your permission."

"He touched me in appropriately," she said. Again. He'd done it again, and this time she'd reported it like Sophia, Lily, and Emma had asked her to do. *We have to start telling adults when they pull this shit,* Lily had said. *It'll never stop unless we do.*

Franco shook his head. "Since when is rubbing your shoulder inappropriate touching? Is that where we are?"

Her hands tried to clench, but she fought them. "If he was trying to rub my shoulder, he missed."

He waved, dismissing her complaint. "You misunderstood his intentions. On a related note, take a seat in the front office. Your mother is on the way with a change of clothes since you've violated the dress code. Once more, and you'll have detention."

She looked down at her outfit. What the entire fuck was he about? "My jeans?"

"They are a little tight." His eyes focused on her groin, and his lip curled. "But no, the problem is with your top. It exposes your collarbones."

She fingered the neckline. Shame crawled over her, and frustration and anger followed. She wanted to rage at him, but defeat curled around her. What was the point?

Her mother brought her baggy blue crew-neck T-shirt, and rolled her eyes when Mackenzie tried to tell her about what happened. "Just go back to class. If you don't learn to let these things go, you'll be unhappy your whole life." She snuck a kiss to Mackenzie's forehead and left.

The office secretary handed her a hall pass back to class. *Dress code violation* was scrawled across the top, icing on the cake that was this week. As she turned the corner to head for her locker, Franco, his normally pasty skin mottled with rage, barreled past her. His two-way radio squawked something about the girls' freshman hall bathroom.

For as long as Mackenzie could remember, she'd looked for the light in people. Everyone she'd ever met had at least a pebble of humanity that deserved compassion and respect. It was rare someone could be so aggressively awful that she wondered if they were even human.

Franco was one. She'd thought she hated him after the way he responded to her complaint about Jake, but since then she'd descended to a new level of revulsion. As of today, he could be drowning in a puddle, and she wouldn't kick him over. Not after what he'd done to Sophia.

"We have to get him fired," she said. Lily, Sophia, and Emma sat in a circle with her on the carpeted floor of her bedroom. Soph pulled her knees to her chest and rocked. The usually diamond-hard pink cloud surrounding her had faded in vibrance. It almost matched her pale shirt.

Em stroked Soph's back, and the multiple rings she wore clinked together in a soothing rhythm. "How?" she asked. "He didn't get fired after he covered up that one rape."

Lily glanced around the circle, her steely aura flexing, and tugged hard on a hank of her black hair. "Social media."

"No! Please don't make this more public," Sophia said. Old tear tracks stained her cheeks, and she dropped her head on her knees. "I feel like this is it. Nothing will ever change. We'll all be stuck with this bullshit forever."

Soft purple blossomed around Emma as she prepared to speak. Mackenzie knew what she would suggest. It was a little crazy and a lot scary, but it was the only thing left to their fledgling group.

"Let's go ask for help in the woods," she said.

They looked to Sophia. Emma's hand stilled with a muffled *clink* on Sophia's back as she furrowed her brow and thought hard. After several tense seconds, she nodded.

Emma snatched the Goddess tarot deck Mackenzie kept in a cheap velveteen scrap on her bedside table. She unfolded the velveteen and smoothed it, shuffled the cards, and dealt three, face up. She chewed her thumb with her head lowered, and her bright red hair slowly fell to curtain her face.

The color in the room changed to a dusky rose as the sun escaped the day, and weird shadows spread across the cards on the scrap, undulating like the smoke from the sandalwood incense burning on her dresser. Mackenzie shivered. It was only the effect of long shadows, but it was creepy as fuck. "What do they say?" she asked.

Lily had taken up rubbing Sophia's back in large, smooth circles, but her eyes darted to look at Mackenzie. They were filled with dread and excitement and a relentless need for Franco's head on a stick. Mackenzie knew that need.

Emma laid the deck of cards beside the cloth, sat back on her heels, and tucked her hair behind her ears. "Ukemochi for past." She glanced at Sophia, who kept her head on her knees. "The Wawalak for present. And King of Swords for what we do next." Her words were flat and resigned.

"So, you think that's a yes?" Mackenzie bit her lip. Waited for the inevitable. The creepy feeling hadn't left, and it gave the moment a weird sense of importance, like they were planning something they could never come back from.

Emma nodded.

"Definitely." Lily's voice shook.

Mackenzie eyed the stack of unused tarot cards. She itched with the need to pluck the next and see what it said.

Her lips pinched, Emma gazed at Mackenzie. Mackenzie gave a quick nod of solidarity and support. Nobody wanted to go, but they'd do it. They'd do anything for Sophia. They'd do anything for each other.

Sophia's breath caught.

"We'll go tonight," Emma said.

Mackenzie stashed the cards behind the small Persephone statue by her rumpled twin bed.

When the Lyft driver dropped them at the trailhead, the woman called out the window, "Are you gals sure this is the right place?"

Emma waved. "We'll be fine, thanks."

"Those freaks live out there somewhere," the driver said. "Heard it's like a witch cult or something." She paused, stretched her head out the window, and eyed them. "Y'all aren't into that, are you?"

Emma stepped closer, leaned in, and smiled. "You can go. We're all right. Really."

The woman shook her head as if bemused. She sank back behind the steering wheel and drove away, though the car hesitated before it turned onto the main road.

Mackenzie gripped Sophia's soft hand when Emma turned to face the trail. Sophia squeezed twice in quick succession, an old signal they'd come up with when they were in fourth grade, something they'd had to use more than a few times on the playground, at the bus stop, and even in Sophia's own home before her father had accepted her. Two meant she was okay. One sustained squeeze meant she needed help.

"Ready?" Emma asked.

Rumor at school said it was a three-day walk to the commune and the trail was beset by demons and monsters, but Google's satellite images showed it was only a mile into the woods. Google couldn't see how far the trails wound or which ones to take or which had demons to avoid, but Lily could find a cotton ball in a blizzard. She'd had the uncanny skill for the year-plus they'd known her, even on her first day of school when Emma gave her a tour through their labyrinthine halls. She said Lily could have done it on her own and had the lay of the school within ten minutes.

"I swallowed a magnet when I was a baby," she'd told them not long after they'd befriended her. "The doctors thought it might kill me, but it gave me useless superpowers instead."

They'd all laughed, but Mackenzie had spent weeks considering other objects that might give up their power when swallowed.

Even with Lily's ability to navigate anywhere, it took over an hour to find the commune. A thick silence blanketed the clearing. Sophia's flashlight barely provided enough light to see their way through the smattering of tents that reeked of unwashed bodies, but she led them to the only tent with a lamp flickering against the dark.

As they approached, a young woman maybe a year or two out of high school emerged from the lamplit tent like she'd expected them. Her unkempt hair fell nearly to her waist, and she wore ceremonial robes like the ones Mackenzie had seen in the metaphysical bookstore in town. They looked even more ridiculous on a real person than they did on the mannequin. As the woman walked toward them, bells clinked and tinkled.

Her lips stretched in a wide grin, and a hue the shade of old blood and the texture of glass shards enveloped her. “Nobody’s here. You should go back.”

Mackenzie balled her fists, ready to fight, ready to steal what they needed.

Emma darted a look at Sophia, but Lily spoke up first. “We came for help.”

“You won’t get that here,” the woman whispered, her fierce grin never wavering, her eyes shining.

Emma stepped back and grasped Mackenzie’s wrist. “She’s right. We should go.”

“No. We came all this way, Em,” Mackenzie whispered, yanking her wrist away. “The cards said—” But Emma turned and hurried toward the trailhead.

Mackenzie glanced at Sophia, whose look of hopelessness broke her heart. Lily looked angry and confused, and Mackenzie clenched her fists tighter. She spun back toward the crazy woman, but the cloud around her had gone dark, dark like it was bottomless. She could take this woman, but not alone. They needed to get her to tell them … something. Anything that might help. She ran after the retreating girls. Behind them, bells tinkled until they were muffled behind a tent flap.

When they’d made it a short way down the trail, Mackenzie said, “I’m serious. What the hell? We need her to help us.” But Emma shushed her violently.

Mackenzie wanted to punch a tree. They’d read the cards. They’d all agreed. They’d made the trek to the middle of the woods to find weirdos everyone was afraid of, and now they’d just turn around and leave? Emma could appoint herself their leader, but she couldn’t run them over, couldn’t dictate what they’d do.

Mackenzie grasped Emma’s shoulder to stop her and forced her to face them.

“What the fuck?” was all she could bite out around her anger.

"Turn your flashlight off, Sophia," Emma said in a low, tight voice, "unless you'd rather run all the way back to the road." She pulled a hair band from her jeans pocket and pulled her red hair away from the beads of sweat now lining her face. Even in the dark, Mackenzie could see the pulsating color around her. Normally dark purple, now it was a sickly lavender.

An icy chill filled the air around the group, cooling Mackenzie's anger a few degrees. The flashlight clicked off, and Emma whispered, "Keep walking."

"What's wrong?" Lily's voice barely rose over the soft sounds of their footsteps in fallen leaves.

Emma remained quiet for long seconds. "The woman at the camp had a chain around her ankle. Lily, which way?"

Lily stared at the forked road looming before them and said nothing.

"What do you mean, she had a chain?" Mackenzie asked, but then she remembered the sound of bells. Or, not bells.

"You could see it coming from the back of her robe. She was attached to something in the tent. Lily?"

Sophia shifted from foot to foot. "I have to pee. Please hurry."

Lily huffed. "I'm not sure. Just go pee."

"Quiet, though," Emma said. Light from the sliver of moon above the canopy of leaves glinted on her hair, making the red look more purple.

Sophia's eyes sparkled like they were wet with tears. Mackenzie took her hand. "It's okay. We'll turn around."

Sophia hesitated, but then gave a quick double-squeeze and moved toward the trees at the side of the trail.

"Don't go too far, Soph," Emma said.

They turned away as promised and huddled close while they waited.

"What's going on, Lily?" Emma murmured. "I thought you could get us out of here."

"I don't know," she whispered. "I remember we came in on the right fork, but my Spidey sense says to go left. I think. I don't know."

Mackenzie closed her eyes and inhaled some fresh night air, forcing herself to calm down.

Emma and Lily debated which way they should go, but Mackenzie tuned them out, intent on listening for Sophia to return. She couldn't hear anything, though. No sound of movement and not the patter of urine hitting forest floor. For a second, panic threatened to overwhelm her, and she had to force herself not to glance back to make sure Sophia was still there, trying her damnedest to pee in an alien place.

Mackenzie had a terrible feeling their friend wouldn't recover from the bullying and threats anytime soon and that things would get worse.

She was about to call out to her when Sophia grabbed her upper arm. Mackenzie exhaled with relief and turned to smile at her. But it wasn't Sophia standing there.

An old woman, her scraggly hair failing to conceal the rage on her face, glared at her with beady black eyes.

Lily gasped behind Mackenzie, and the sounds of stumbling and cursing echoed through the trees around them.

The woman's tight grip pinched hard enough to sting her skin, but instead of shrinking away as she wanted to do, Mackenzie turned into the woman and met her gaze, unblinking and direct.

The woman bared her teeth. "They see through the veil." Her loamy breath wafted over Mackenzie. Then she shifted and yanked Sophia, whom she held with her left hand wrapped tight around the girl's skinny arm. "They walk between the worlds."

She released them, and Mackenzie gasped as her legs went numb and weak. She dropped to the ground, and a sharp pain hit her upper thigh. Sophia fell, too, but her wide-eyed expression didn't falter with her hard landing. Mackenzie's leg screamed as a rock dug into the muscle, but she couldn't move to relieve the pain. She couldn't move at all. Her heart beat hard and fast, and she panted with the attempt to make her body respond and do something, help them stand, get her friends away from the danger.

The old woman stepped away from her and Sophia and toward Lily and Emma. Emma squeaked like she was trying and failing to scream, but neither girl moved, not even when the woman grabbed them. "They see the threads. And they cut them."

"You're hurting me," Emma said through clenched teeth, her words halting and forced. "Let me go before I cut you, old lady." But she didn't move. Mackenzie knew she couldn't, not while the old woman had them.

"I'm not the one, tiny human," she said, and then she laughed and released the girls. Emma and Lily dropped to the ground, too, Lily grunting when she landed on her back.

Mackenzie forced herself to slow her breathing and to focus her will. She'd never walk again, she was sure, if she didn't get up right then. Her legs tingled, and she rolled off the rock digging into her thigh. She forced herself to her feet, though her legs shook with the effort. She wasn't sure what she meant to do, but they needed to leave before this crazy bitch did something, and before someone else found them.

The woman spun as Mackenzie stood and straightened, and as she did, she seemed to grow six inches, then a foot. Mackenzie opened her mouth to yell, but the woman grabbed her by the neck and squeezed so tight Mackenzie knew she'd pass out. She flailed and punched when the old lady pulled her close and lifted her until they were face to face, noses touching. Her fists never seemed to land, though.

"You came for help, but the gods don't give a shit about you. Nobody does. So here is my gift to you. You are cursed, and only you can break the curse." The woman's rich, soil-scented breath caked the inside of Mackenzie's mouth. When the woman dropped her and she was able to inhale at last, she tasted it all the way down her throat, like she'd swallowed a clod of dirt. "No prisoners. No mercy. No more chains."

Mackenzie's throat spasmed, threatening to close again. She coughed and spat and rubbed the protesting muscles. Vaguely, she could hear her friends crying around her, and all she could think was they'd best be quiet before the commune people came for them and chained them inside the tents.

But the woman had disappeared. As soon as Mackenzie caught her breath and her strength returned with another rush of adrenaline, she stood, took a long and deep breath, gathered their group. Lily eventually led them out of the woods to the main road. While they huddled by a light post, she called up a Lyft.

"Guys, she cursed us," Sophia said and pulled Lily closer to her. "I'm sorry I said we should come."

"No," Mackenzie whispered, reaching out to join Soph and Lily in a hug, and their colors combined into a shimmering mermaid pink around her. "No, she didn't. We're fine. We had a crazy as shit adventure. That's all." Emma looked shell-shocked, and her color was still a dim lavender. Mackenzie reached out to tug her into their fold.

But she couldn't stop wondering if the woman really had cursed them. Or maybe she was only pointing out the obvious—they were cursed before they ever arrived.

The fear and, worse, the disappointment of leaving with less than they'd had before they started ate at Mackenzie all night. Sophia went fetal on the large pallet they'd made on the floor of Mackenzie's room, and silent sobs jerked her body. Everyone else curled around her and comforted her until the sun cracked open the morning.

They each looked like death when they got up and quietly folded the blankets they'd used. Lily tugged at her hair, her eyes distant and her shoulders slumped. Em didn't even bother running her fingers through her red tangles, and she left looking like she wore a badly abused clown's wig. Sophia put on a fake smile and thanked Mackenzie's mom for letting them stay the night. She almost sounded convincing.

When Lily and Em had gone, too, Mackenzie dug the tarot card from the top of the pile—the next card in the draw, the one to signify the consequences of their quest—and was not surprised to find graying, sagging skies, blood-washed hills, and turbulent waters following a boat stabbed through by six swords.

On Monday, Lily was absent. Emma and Sophia looked worse than they had Saturday morning. None of them had called or texted the rest of the weekend. Mackenzie had avoided them because she'd woken from sleep chilled and with the taste of earth in her mouth. She wondered if they'd also had nightmares.

After lunch, Mackenzie and Emma escorted Sophia to the nurse's office so she could use the restroom in peace. They waited outside for their friend to finish her business.

"What's wrong with Lily?" Em asked.

"No idea. I haven't heard from her," Mackenzie said. She fidgeted with her necklace. "Did she say anything to you?"

Em shook her head.

When the sound of familiar voices drifted around the corner, they froze and stared at each other.

"I saw him go this way. I figured you'd wanna know," said a boy whose deepening voice hadn't quite committed to an octave.

"I appreciate your diligence," said a man whose gravelly voice Mackenzie recognized.

Franco, she mouthed to Emma, who nodded and faded back against the wall. She closed her eyes, and her fingers fluttered like she was playing a piano.

When Mr. Franco and Jake rounded the corner, they stopped. The principal straightened, propped his hands on his hips, and studied Mackenzie.

"Where is he?" He glanced at the nurse, visible through the door at her desk. "Did he go in there?"

Mackenzie shifted her eyes away, ready to answer truthfully and as minimally as she could, but Emma's fluttering fingers caught her attention. She thought of the six of swords in her pocket, and something shifted in her. She snapped her gaze back to Franco and let her direct stare bore into him for a long moment, an act she should—normally would—have found uncomfortable.

"Answer me, young lady," Franco said. Jake smirked behind him.

Mackenzie propped her hands on her own hips to mimic the man's posture. "Who?" she asked.

"You know who." His voice dropped in pitch. His cheek twitched, and the vein in his forehead throbbed like it ticked down toward an eventual aneurysm.

"Afraid I don't," she said. "Sir."

He narrowed his eyes and sneered. "I won't stand for attitude, young lady. Did Zachary go in there?"

"I don't know a Zachary, but I haven't seen any guys this way until now. If you're curious, you could always ask the nurse. She's right inside." A thrill filled her, only intensifying when Jake glowered at her from his position behind Franco. Mackenzie had never spoken like this to someone in charge. Not to her parents. Certainly not to teachers or a principal.

The nurse appeared in the door, and a scowl darkened her face. The bell rang then, and a cascade of students poured through the classroom doors along the hall.

"Mr. Franco, could I speak to you in your office?" the nurse asked. "It's important." She gestured at the man, and for a second, both his eyes and his mouth opened wide as if he would object. His blotchy cheeks darkened to an unhealthy maroon. Behind Mackenzie, Emma whispered something, and Franco finally relented and let himself be led away. Sophia darted from the nurse's office as soon as the crowd had swallowed the principal.

Mackenzie grabbed her backpack and melted away from the group with a sigh of relief. She felt light on her feet, a little giddy, after surviving that confrontation. But as Jake watched her go, his lips parted. His tongue flicked out to moisten his lips in a deliberate way he probably meant to be provocative and threatening but that came off as sluggishly reptilian. She barked a laugh at him as she turned the corner and leaned against the wall to wait until Emma and Sophia hurried around. They took off again, Emma and Mackenzie flanking their vulnerable friend.

Once Mackenzie made it to her next class, the adrenaline rush wore off, and her hands shook. She'd stood up to a pack of bullies and hadn't backed down. She felt powerful. It was probably a first in her life, certainly the first she could remember.

Later, as she stood with her back against the painted cement block wall, waiting for dismissal at seventh period, she reveled in the blazing heat emanating from her throat to her extremities and the crown of her head. She felt as if it might overflow, and her skull would blow the top off like a volcano everyone had believed was dormant. The thought of painting the classroom in rage-lava made her very, very happy.

Her joy didn't last long. After dismissal, Jake found her by the buses and pinned her against one. His dick poked her in the leg. "You keep protecting that freak, and we'll take care of you." He jabbed her hard, right on the bruise she still had from the fall on the trail, and she gasped. He grinned at her and darted his tongue out. "Won't that be fun?"

She shoved him, furious and disgusted, and he laughed and started for her again, the red-streaked gray around him reaching toward her, too.

A guy Mackenzie vaguely recognized came around the bus and smacked Jake on the back of his head. "Why you always being an asshole, man?"

Jake laughed like it was a big joke and then walked away with a side-eye glare thrown her way. The guy who'd called him out followed, but as he left, he jerked a nod at her. Maybe he meant to show he had her back, but she'd bet her firstborn he'd want a favor in return.

After three days, Emma and Sophia were absent from school, too. Lily texted Mackenzie. *Dr said I'm faking. FTG.*

Mackenzie had initially felt better rested and more alert on Monday night and Tuesday morning, though the nightmares continued, and she always woke with the taste of forest floor rot. But when her precalculus teacher told her not to bother trying out for the mathlete team because he didn't think she'd hold up to the stress of competition, that strength drained away.

By Wednesday, when she made it to soccer tryouts and didn't perform to her usual standard, the last of her energy guttered like a clogged gas stove. Her name was placed on the second-day tryouts list. Last year, she'd needed only one tryout to make the team. The shame nearly buckled her knees.

As she left the locker room, her backpack slung over her shoulder and her street clothes stuffed in her soccer bag, she overheard Coach Brimley say, "Just an off day. I know she's junior varsity material. Maybe even varsity if she's been practicing. Mac has potential."

The assistant coach, Paulson, a new guy straight out of college, snorted. "Probably it's just that time of the month."

Coach Brimley shrugged as he made marks on the clipboard he held. A vague frown pinched the corner of his mouth.

Mackenzie waited to feel a wave of shame, but instead, a tsunami of rage rose in her, blotting out all but the vision of Coach Brimley—always a great coach and an understanding guy—next to this shit stain of an assistant coach with his self-satisfied laugh. Her feet stopped moving and her arms lost their ability to hold her bags. Everything thumped to the floor. Paulson glanced up at her, and he had the good grace to flush.

She felt his flush in her skin, warming and loosening and sinking deep into her muscles. When she opened her mouth, the words formed in the air outside of her, animated by her exhaled breath, and rushed straight at the assistant coach.

"Men like to mock what they fear, Mr. Paulson. But they still haven't realized how pathetic they look when they show everyone how weak they are." She heard the words, she heard her voice behind them, but she heard something else in there, too. It was older than her, and it was wiser, and it was enraged. The truth in those words filled her with strength she'd needed all week, and if she didn't know better, she'd have said she grew six inches in that moment, nearly towering over the assistant coach.

Coach looked up at her then, his brows drawn close. "What's that, Mac?"

She smiled at him, and her voice returned to her throat. "Sorry about my tryout. I'll be back to myself tomorrow." She swept up her bags, spared a long smile at the still-floundering assistant coach, and left.

There were no nightmares that night.

There was only the old woman in the forest, no longer mocking and sneering but smiling at her in the dreamtime woods with night-blooming flowers rooting in the fecund earth and spreading their petals wide. "No prisoners, no mercy, no chains." But in her dream, the old woman's voice sounded like her own.

The next morning, Mackenzie grabbed the tarot card she'd kept and stuffed it into the middle of the deck. Without thinking, following instinct, she tore a leaf from her classroom copy of *The Great Gatsby*, translated her need into looping words and shapes with a Sharpie, and placed the folded paper under a lodestone. She dropped a coin next to the items and left for school, ready to take the upper hand.

At second period, the kid behind her called her a skank. He laughed, probably because he usually got a rise out of her. But today, he had no power over her. When she looked back at him and his snickering friends, they paused and waited with wide smiles for the next thing they could mock.

"It's a shame about your voice," she said, staring pointedly at his throat. The words formed as they left her mouth and drifted straight to him. He jerked back.

She returned to her work and waited for the kid and his friends to burst into laughter. When they did, the piece of shit who'd called her a skank choked and coughed. “Freak,” he said, but his voice cracked and broke, and he coughed again.

She smiled, knowing that was the last word he’d say for a long time.

Emma, Lily, and Sophia had tried to return to school, but none of them made it longer than a period or two before they were in the nurse’s office and then back home.

By Friday there were rumors of a weird flu affecting a few boys at the school. There were also rumors that the new assistant coach who’d quit on Wednesday was in the hospital, too weak to move or talk or even eat. The kids laughed and joked and said this was the zombie apocalypse, and he was patient zero.

At the first week of the varsity team’s soccer practice, Ms. Hampton, the girls’ basketball coach, came out to run them through drills. “Coach Brimley’s sick,” she told them when they asked after him.

Mackenzie hoped he’d survive what she was certain was coming, but he’d been complicit, so she didn’t hold out much hope.

That weekend, Mackenzie made the rounds of her friends’ houses. Lily was in bed, struggling to stay awake, but she listened intently as Mackenzie pulled a page out of the book and explained what they all needed to do. Lily scribbled something on the paper, and Mackenzie helped her hide the tiny altar they created from it. She took her collection of paper and lodestones covered in palmarosa oil and iron filings to Emma and to Sophia on Saturday.

By Monday, they were all back in class, and intense relief washed over Mackenzie when she saw them laugh together, their separate strong colors melding and growing and taking on the feel of granite. Less than half the school was in attendance, and some classes were combined for lack of substitute teachers. Franco ended up in the hospital, too, and Mackenzie sincerely hoped he wouldn’t survive.

On Tuesday, a girl Mackenzie had never met turned in her seat after morning announcements. "You know how to get it back? That's what everyone's saying."

Mackenzie, deep in her math book, could only stare at the girl. "Get what back?"

The girl glanced at one of the few remaining boys in the room. He looked pasty. "How to get *us* back. Everything they've taken from us." She looked pointedly at the pasty boy and back at Mackenzie. "Everything we could have been."

Mackenzie smiled, and then she shared what she'd learned. As she spoke, she imagined she could smell the soil in the teacher's giant potted monstera filling the room.

By Wednesday, the metaphysical bookstore ran out of lodestones, *The Great Gatsby* had two sad leaves remaining inside its tattered cover, and Emma, Lily, and Sophia joined Mackenzie in blessing girls throughout the school with small altars. They ordered more lodestones to gift to their mothers and grandmothers. They kissed their fathers and grandfathers and offered them tissues when their noses congested.

By Friday, there were laughing rumors of a Hollywood-style government quarantine after the remaining news anchor told her local audience that their city had been affected by a virulent flu. As many of the nice guys as outright assholes had fallen ill, and a scant few men hung tight to their health. News spread quickly through the school that Franco had died the night before, and Mackenzie laughed.

"It's funny," Lily said during lunch. "I've always known exactly where to go, but now I feel safe going." She bit her sandwich and grinned as grape jelly leaked from the edge of the bread, splatting onto the cafeteria table.

Emma reached out to them, and they grasped each other's hands, forming a ring in a lunchroom that reeked of microwave pizza and spilled Pepsi. "Then let's do it. Let's just go."

"Where?" asked Sophia.

"Wherever," said Lily.

Mackenzie squeezed the hands she held, twice in quick succession. "No chains."

During the noisy combined science class, Jake, looking pale and angry, skulked into the room and chose the seat behind Sophia and Mackenzie. He managed to behave for almost the entire period but toward the end said, “Hey, you freak,” loud enough to be heard over the chatter and laughter in the room. His voice was cracked and brittle, and Mackenzie was sure his rage was the only thing animating him. She could hardly see any color around him at all.

Sophia turned around in her seat, slowly and confidently, her back straight without being rigid, her chin up, her wild blond curls glowing. Jake jerked up so fast, Mackenzie thought he’d touched a live wire.

“Why aren’t you dead?” Sophia asked. The room quieted.

“Jesus,” he whispered. He shifted his eyes between Sophia and her. Mackenzie smiled wide at him, and his eyes grew in time with her mouth. “Jesus, Mary, and Joseph.”

“Pray all you want,” Mackenzie said. “Your god doesn’t give a shit about you.”

Sophia grinned and waggled her eyebrows at Mackenzie. Her face flushed with confidence. Her eyes glittered. She pulled a tarot card from her pocket and laid it carefully in front of Jake. He stared at the image of men falling to their deaths from a lightning-struck tower. Sweat beaded along his hairline and trickled down his face. A sour smell emanated from him.

Death. He smelled like the death he saw in the card.

Her mouth filled with the rich flavor of dark forest earth, of rot and verdant roots, and she swallowed it. Words, fully gestated, formed just inside her mouth and rushed straight at Jake.

“Don’t worry. We’ll take care of you, just like we took care of Franco and all the other guys,” Mackenzie told him. “Won’t that be fun?”

He twitched as the words hit him, but then he froze in his seat. Only his eyes moved, wide and shiny, flicking between all the girls in the classroom as they gathered in a circle around him.

HAVE ME FOR DINNER

by
Nikki Hopeman

Astrid's stomach made the sounds of a singing whale. Damn, she was hungry. She grabbed her midsection, tried to massage her belly into silence. That would be embarrassing in a meeting.

She pushed the button for the elevator in the parking garage and waited. How long had it been? She'd been trying hard to be good, to not indulge … but she couldn't put it off much longer.

The elevator indicator dinged. She straightened her beige pencil skirt and readjusted the strap of her messenger bag on her shoulder before she stepped into the waiting car.

"Hey! Hold that! Hey, gorgeous! You!"

She groaned and punched the open-door button. She popped her head through the doors to see who was yelling, although she had a good guess. A tall, handsome, well-dressed man waved at her from two rows of cars away. He'd managed to be at the elevator around the same time as her for the last month, and it was obvious what he was after. She rolled her eyes but kept her finger on the button.

You catch more flies with honey, she told herself. She'd also learned it was best not to create drama. Especially not with her current hunger level.

After several seconds, he hopped into the elevator. He was just slightly winded from his trot across the garage, and he made a show of flexing his muscles under his button-down shirt.

"Whew," he said, with a white-toothed grin. "Just in time."

No, you were late, she thought, but didn't say it out loud. Usually he met her right as she got on the elevator. His suit was a size or so too small—better to show off his weightlifting prowess, she guessed—and he stood at least four inches taller than her.

"Thirty-eight, right?"

"Good memory, sweets."

She sighed softly and pressed thirty-eight and forty, her floor. Another interminable ride with him. He was leaning toward her and his breath smelled like sweaty socks, wet and musky on her face.

She felt him staring and glanced over. She wasn't wrong. His leering gaze roamed her legs and ass.

Astrid's skirt reached just below her knees, a modest length, completely appropriate office attire, and not too tight. Her blouse was both long-sleeved and high-necked. There was nothing suggestive about her dress.

His gaze traveled up her legs to her breasts and then to her face. She studiously avoided eye contact and tried not to squirm. She wished she'd worn her blazer instead of carrying it.

"Don't you work for Hancock and Anderson?"

She was surprised he could talk through the flexing and grinning. "I do. I don't think we've been introduced."

"No, but I've seen you around." He put a hand out, palm up. "I'm Frank Hobart, with Hobart Realty."

She peered at the sheen of his sweaty palm, mentally shuddered, and gritted her teeth as she slid her hand into his. "Astrid."

He grasped her hand, caressing her fingers and licked his lips. "Just Astrid?"

"Just Astrid."

He released her hand and she tried not to wipe it on the blazer she had over her arm.

The elevator bounced once before it stopped on thirty-eight. He put a foot in front of the sliding doors. "See you around, Astrid."

His stare bored into her, penetrating. Her stomach knotted. "Uh. Sure. Frank."

Another wide, smarmy grin. He continued to stand there, holding the door, keeping her captive in the elevator car. An awkward pause ensued in which his gaze swept up and down her legs.

"Well, I should be headed to my floor," she said.

"Okay, but this isn't the last you'll see of me." He finally sauntered out of the car and released the doors.

She gave him a tight smile as the doors closed and transported her the last two floors. She knew who he was and was sure he knew her, too. He'd practically been stalking her, like a coyote after a rabbit, for weeks now.

When the lift reached her floor, the doors slid open and finally freed her. The soothing light blue of the familiar hallway greeted her. She walked into her tiny office— paralegals weren't given a ton of space, and she didn't mind—and put her bag on the chair beside her desk.

She sat in her swivel-chair and opened the calendar on her computer. Tomorrow was a full day in depositions with her boss and she had to prepare.

Her stomach mooed a complaint and she groaned a little. Today was Thursday. She could make it to Friday night.

"Morning, Astrid." Astrid's boss, Kristen, the Hancock half of the legal partnership, walked past her office on her way to her own, just down the hall, the crisp click of her stilettos on the tile punctuating her words.

"Morning, Kristen. Getting things ready for the depositions tomorrow."

"Excellent, thanks. You're the best."

Astrid spent the morning going over the numerous emails they'd be entering into evidence against a landlord who'd illegally evicted one of their clients.

"We're headed out to lunch." Kristen stopped at the door of Astrid's office. "You coming?"

"No, thanks. I'm just going to barrel through these emails."

Kristen peered at her, frowning. "You sure?"

"Yeah. I have… dinner plans for tomorrow night."

Kristen's puzzled expression cleared. "Okay. See you in an hour."

The rest of Astrid's day went as well as could be expected, except for the gnawing and gnashing in her gut. She did her best to ignore it and keeping busy helped.

The alarm on her phone dinged at five o'clock. She slapped at it until it stopped ringing, then finished up the email she was highlighting.

She pulled herself out of her chair and stretched, realizing she hadn't even taken a break to walk. The muscles of her neck were tight and sore, and she rolled her head gently, loosening them. Other cramped muscles complained, but her stomach yelled the loudest.

"Oh, stop," she told it. "I can't do anything about you until tomorrow night."

She packed her laptop and the remaining hard-copy evidentiary emails into her bag and entered the hallway. "Hey, I'm headed home," she called.

Voices responded with the obligatory "see yous" and "good nights" as Astrid pushed the elevator button.

The doors opened, revealing Frank Hobart inside the car. She did her best to control her facial expression as she stepped in.

"Well, imagine seeing you here." He his leer was grating. He'd changed into athletic pants—again, too small—and a tight T-shirt.

"Imagine. I thought you worked on thirty-eight."

"I was up on forty-three in the gym."

Astrid took a deep breath and blinked slowly, pressing her eyelids together tightly to stop her eyebrows from rising. "Really? That's dedication."

His gaze lingered on her neck, searing her with its intensity, but wouldn't meet her eyes. "I like to stay fit. Helps with so many things."

Did she imagine a slight hip thrust when he said that?

"I'm a runner myself."

The brute made a show of checking out her calves. "I bet you are. I ran in high school." He nodded, pushed out his chest. "Held my high school's four-hundred-meter dash record until 2006. Track-and-field star."

"I bet you were." *Shit*. That'd come out a little snarky.

He looked at her with suspicion.

"I mean, you still have a runner's physique, that's for sure," she said.

Goddamn it. If she jammed her foot any further past her lips, she'd choke.

His eyes sparkled and he winked at her. "If you like what you see, baby, we can arrange for you to have a taste."

She responded carefully. "I'm sure you're very busy with work."

"Work's very important, but so is play." He shifted closer to her.

She backed into the corner of the lift and decided a change of subject would be wise. "You're in realty, right?"

He seemed to ease off a little. "I take my job very seriously. I'm helping to build this city."

She nodded. "Important work."

"It sure is," he said. "What do you do up on forty?"

"Oh, I'm just a paralegal. I do legal research for the attorneys."

That seemed to satisfy him. "Assistant. That's good."

The elevator bounced and stopped at the garage level. The doors opened and he gallantly put himself in the path of the doors to hold them open for Astrid.

She squeezed past him, and felt his hand graze her ass and thigh. "Thank you."

"I'll walk you to your car."

"No, really that's—-"

"Nonsense." He followed her to her car, a nondescript sedan. "You never know who you'll run into in this garage."

Yeah, assholes like you.

"Well, thanks for seeing me to my car so safely." She pulled her keys from her bag. "I have to get home."

"I'll see you tomorrow, Astrid." He stuck his hand out again, and after a moment's hesitation, she put her hand in his. He caressed her fingers one more time, thumb rubbing her knuckles and sliding up to her wrist.

When he started to lean forward, she was afraid he would kiss her hand. She dropped her bag on the concrete, which allowed her to pull free. He retrieved it for her as she pressed the button to unlock her car, and after accepting her bag, she got in. She gritted her teeth and suppressed the urge to lock the doors right away. The muscle-bound swine stood next to her parking space until she'd driven around the corner of the garage.

So. Gross. She shuddered. *I need a shower. With a lot of soap.* But the encounter cinched things for her. Friday night couldn't come fast enough.

The next morning, Astrid was sure to be right on time. She exited her car and sauntered to the elevator, looking for Frank. When the indicator dinged with Frank nowhere in sight, she released a tense breath and waited for the doors to open. She gasped when they did.

Frank had a younger woman pinned in the corner of the lift car. She was small and he towered over her, nuzzling her ear and groping at her chest.

Her eyes met Astrid's—eyes filled with terror and tears.

Her fury rose with a heat that threatened to boil over.

"Good morning, Frank." The words came out of her mouth silky as a negligee but tinged with a hardness she couldn't suppress.

He took a step back from the cowering woman and grinned. His face was flushed, and the hard bulge in his pants was on full display. "Morning, Astrid."

"So, what's going on here?" she asked, moving toward him, her arm brushing his lightly.

If he grins any wider, his face will split in two.

"Nothing at all! I just needed to get something from my car. Can you hold the door for me?" It was more of an order than a request.

"Sure, Frank," she purred. "I'd be glad to."

He jogged a couple aisles over, his shoes tapping a fading cadence on the concrete floor.

Astrid quickly exited the elevator when Frank was out of sight. "Go. Take this one. I'll call another."

Tears spilled onto the younger woman's cheeks. "Thanks so much."

"This isn't the first time, is it?"

She shook her head, her cheeks flushing, and refused to meet Astrid's eyes.

"Don't worry," Astrid said, hearing the venom in her own voice. "I'll take care of him."

Confusion replaced the terror in the woman's eyes. "Don't let him get you alone." Fresh tears. "He likes to hurt us."

Astrid shook her head. "Just go."

She watched relief flood across the other woman's face as the doors of the elevator closed. Her resolve turned into granite. She pushed the call button and the doors of the adjacent car opened almost immediately.

After a few minutes, the blare of a car alarm filled the air, and Frank trotted back. Empty-handed.

"Where's Amy?" He peered around and had the audacity to look irritated.

Astrid could almost hear his mind shouting, *Cock tease. Slut. Whore!*

"She said she was very late to run an errand. I let her take that elevator." Astrid glanced down at his empty hands. "You needed to get something?"

"It's not there. Must be upstairs after all."

Jesus, could you be more transparent? She guessed his IQ score was on par with a slug. No, too high.

"Too bad." She licked and gently bit her bottom lip. "Could have saved yourself a trip."

"But then I would have missed you," he said, moving toward her and leaning in too close.

She slid her bag between her and Frank, while maintaining eye contact.

"We couldn't have that, could we?"

"No, we couldn't." His breath was hot. He needed a Tic Tac. "And I just gotta say, babe, you look . . . amazing today."

She'd dressed very deliberately this morning. Professionally, of course. Couldn't be too obvious, but just enough to make Frank think she was game. Her black skirt was a little shorter than her pencil skirt, and her semi-sheer blouse had a low-cut neckline. She'd worn her hair in loose, soft curls, and had a pair of killer Manolos on her feet. They lifted her ass and accentuated her curves.

She could almost hear him salivating and watched the tip of his tongue flick out of his mouth to wet his lips.

"Thank you." She pushed the button for forty. "Thirty-eight?"

He just nodded, his hot gaze consuming her. He reached out and fingered one of her long curls.

Her stomach rumbled, and she was glad of the elevator noise to cover it. She sniffed the air and smelled testosterone, sweat, and lust. A glance at his eyes, which were focused on her cleavage, showed dilated pupils.

She exhaled deeply and heard him inhale her scent. The tempo of his breath increased, and his neck muscles flexed. He loosened his tie.

The elevator dinged to a stop at thirty-eight.

He didn't move.

"Frank? This is your stop."

He grabbed her arm, roughly pulled her close, then pinned her against a wall, rubbing his erection against her hip.

"Frank. We're on your floor." She pitched her voice low and hard.

He seemed to shake himself loose, like a dog, and came around again. "What? Oh, my floor."

He backed away from her reluctantly, rubbing his crotch. "You, uh, you have a good day, Astrid."

She smiled. "You, too Frank."

His leering stare never left her as the doors closed.

In her office, Astrid put her hair in a low bun and pulled on her blazer. She swapped the Manolos for flats and organized all the exhibits she and Kristen would be entering into evidence as part of the deposition.

Lauren, the Anderson part of Hancock and Anderson, knocked on the door jamb to Astrid's office. "Good luck today." She eyed Astrid's shirt and the Manolos on the floor by the desk. She gave Astrid a small, sly smile. "Good luck with the whole day."

Astrid smiled back. "Thanks, boss."

The elevator dinged, and Astrid ran out to get the court reporter settled. She knew him well and was glad to see him. He was a rather bland guy who treated all of the women in the practice with respect.

Now, anyway.

The deposition went well. They'd extracted some useful information out of the landlord, and both decided the man was a dick. Kristen took dibs on saving his address, with a smile and lick of her lips.

Kristen left early to file paperwork with the county. "Have a great weekend," she'd said, with a smile. "I'm jealous."

The landlord hadn't left the firm until nearly five o'clock. Astrid settled things with the super pleasant court reporter, saw him out, then hurried back to her office. She exchanged the flats for the Manolos, freed her hair from the bun, and put her blazer on the back of her chair.

She sniffed the air. The scent of Frank, sweaty and horny, washed over her, and she knew he would be riding down in the elevator soon. Her stomach wailed in agony

She grabbed her bag and dashed for the elevator.

Ding!

The doors slid open and there was Frank, panting like he'd already been running. His suit was disheveled, and he'd removed his tie, unbuttoning his shirt low enough to show her a fine patch of dark, curly hair.

His Adam's apple bobbed when he swallowed. "Hi, Astrid."

She stepped into the elevator, brushing him lightly at the hip and heard a low groan. "Imagine meeting you here, Frank."

"Yeah," he whispered, reaching out toward her, grasping the air.

The elevator doors closed, and the car began its downward descent. He just stood and stared at her. She smiled languidly and leaned against the wall of the car. "So, any plans for this weekend?"

He blinked, blinked again. “No, I don’t think so.” He shook his head. “Wait, I think I’m supposed to see my kids.”

Kids. “You have kids?”

“Yeah, uh, two daughters.”

Her temper rose a little. “Those girls don’t know how lucky they’re going to be.”

He frowned a little, “What?”

“Just that you’re going to take good care of them, Frank.”

He smiled. “Yeah, I am.”

She leaned toward him. “Frank, would you like to have dinner with me tonight?”

A look of uninhibited exhilaration passed across his face. “Oh yeah, Astrid. I would love to have dinner with you tonight.”

She leaned in even closer, grazed her fingers over the front of his trousers. “Frank.”

“Uh huh.”

“Frank, would you like me to have you for dinner tonight?”

She was sure he’d fall over, but he remained on his feet. “Yes, Astrid,” he breathed on her and squeezed her breast. “I would love for you to have me for dinner tonight.”

The elevator stopped. Astrid backed away from Frank. “You’ll need to meet me at my place.” She bit her bottom lip and lowered her eyelashes.

His eyes never left her face. “Anything you say.”

“Give me your phone.” She took it from him, entered her address in the maps app, and rerouted him slightly to give herself just a few minutes before he would arrive. “Here, follow the directions and meet me there.”

She turned away and walked to her car, emphasizing the seductive swing of her hips. “Don’t be late,” she called over her shoulder.

Astrid arrived back at her house when the sun was still barely above the horizon. The small Tudor sat back from the road on several acres of wooded property. She had plenty of privacy.

She went inside to prepare.

The sound of tires crunching on gravel reached her ears just after the scent of Frank's lust wafted in on a breeze. She heard his car door open and close, with no indicating beep that he'd locked it.

When he came to the door, she was waiting. She'd stripped down to a sheer black negligee, her long legs encased in thigh-high stockings. She still wore the Manolos.

He came in the door with no hesitation and grabbed her around the waist. He buried his face between her breasts and breathed deep before groaning and licking her cleavage with a wet tongue. He squeezed her breasts to his face. She pulled away from him. His pupils were wide and dilated, and more than a little glazed.

"Come."

He followed her toward the bedroom. Once inside, she guided him to the bed and down onto the rubber sheet. By the light of candles, she undressed him, threw his clothes on the floor near the wall. He pawed at her bra and lace panties in an attempt to get them off, drool dribbling free from one corner of his mouth.

"Frank." She leaned over so his face was at her neck.

He moaned.

"Frank."

With an effort, he tore himself away from licking her shoulder. "What?"

"Don't you remember?"

"What? Remember what?"

"You said I could have you for dinner."

His eyes momentarily cleared, but she was on him before he could think too hard. She straddled his waist, grinding into his erection. She pulled a filleting knife from under the pillow and sliced two vertical slits into his neck. Blood spurted out of the wounds and Frank dropped back onto the bed, clutching at her hips, his mouth working silently, struggling.

"What, Frank?"

"Please…" he croaked.

"Please what, Frank?"

"Please have me for dinner."

She purred and dropped to drink deeply.

The Saturday morning sun rose bright. Sunshine streamed through the windows, casting a yellow haze on the carnage in the bedroom.

There was no trace of Frank, save for his clothes and shoes in a heap on the floor.

And the grisly mess on the floor.

Astrid lay naked on the bed, listless, her belly huge, her hunger sated. When the sunlight touched her, she roused.

After a very long, very hot shower, she pulled on a robe and tied it around her giant belly as best she could.

She put her wet hair up in a bun on top of her head and arranged a sheet mask over her face. Honeysuckle scent. She inspected her cuticles and thought it was time for a fresh manicure. After slathering body lotion all over, she removed the sheet mask and gently patted the excess serum into her skin.

Back in the bedroom, she sighed at the mess and got to work. She cleaned up and shoved the dirty rags in a box to be burned later.

Outside, she unrolled a hose and dropped it into the bedroom through the window. She lumbered back around the house and into the bedroom, where she hosed off the walls and rubber sheet. The water, thick with blood and other body fluids, ran into a drain located under the bed.

She hosed down the last meaty bits of her meal, made sure all the dirty water was cleaned from the floor and running into the septic tank.

The cleaning tired her, but she had other things to do. She picked up Frank's clothes and took them to her washing machine. She dropped them in with some extra detergent to rid them of the scent of blood and lust.

While they washed, she made herself tea. She couldn't appreciate regular food unless she'd truly eaten recently, so it made her feel better to know that for the next few months she'd eat like a regular person. She smeared butter on a piece of toast and munched happily.

Her belly started to roll. She shifted uncomfortably in her seat. "Settle down, Frank."

The washing machine dinged, and she moved Frank's clothes into the dryer.

A push on her bladder woke her. The living room was dark. The robe had come untied while she napped, and she watched a hand press outward from inside her belly.

"Fine, fine."

She got up and went to the bathroom to pee, belly shifting so much it nearly sent her off balance. She felt the first serious waves of contractions while on the toilet. The last wave took her, and she grabbed the counter and grunted through it. She had to make it back to the bedroom.

She left the robe in the bathroom and waddled to the bedroom, back to the rubber-covered bed. A contraction tore through her body, forcing her to grab the headboard. She sidled onto the bed through the pain, on her knees, still grasping the headboard. She gritted her teeth and felt another wave.

The contractions came steadily, one after another until she felt like she was afloat on a sea of agony. Again and again, the waves ebbed and flowed over her, leaving her groaning and shaking.

Finally, she felt a release, and saw bloody liquid flood from her vagina. She pulled herself to a squatting position over the rubber sheet and began to push, working with each compression to expel the thing inside.

Her body knew exactly what to do, and within four or five pushes, a red mass, roughly the size of a fresh honeydew, dropped from between her legs onto the sheet with a wet squelch.

She sat back, breathing heavily, and watched as the mass began to gain a form. It pulsed and oozed, grew and unfolded.

As it increased in size, features became apparent. An arm flopped onto the bed from a side, and a face, with mouth open in a silent scream, emerged from the top. In jerky motions, the mass unfurled itself into the shape of a man.

It lay on the bed, gasping for breath. Astrid moved closer to the form, gently touched its brow, and offered her breast. It suckled and gulped greedily, hands fisting and unfisting as if trying to remember the movement.

She settled next to the man-thing on the bed and closed her eyes.

She was up before the sun in the morning. The Frank-thing on the bed looked human again, or as much as Frank would ever look human. She showered, quickly this time, and took his clothes out of the dryer. She ran a quick iron over them, making them look better than they had when he arrived, and took them into the bedroom.

She poked him. “Frank.”

His eyes opened. He blinked at her. “Astrid?”

“Yes. You need to leave.”

“Why am I here? How did I get here?”

“You’re here because I had you for dinner and made you again.”

Silence.

She stifled a laugh. “It’s okay, you won’t remember any of this.”

"I won't?"

"No, and you won't remember the Frank you used to be, either, okay?"

"Okay."

"Now you're Frank Hobart, the nice guy who respects others and especially women, right?"

"Right."

"Because a woman has given you life twice now, Frank."

"Twice. Yep."

She handed him his clothes. "Wash yourself and get your clothes on. Then leave. I have to clean up after you. Again."

"Okay."

Monday morning Astrid got out of her car in the parking garage and headed for the elevator. She heard someone behind her.

Frank fumbled with his keys. "Good morning," he said when they reached the elevator.

"Good morning. How was your weekend?"

"It was …" He shook his head. "It was good."

"I'm glad to hear it."

"Fortieth floor, right?"

"Yes, thanks."

They rode up in silence. The elevator stopped at thirty-eight and Frank got out. He paused. "Have a great day …" He looked confused.

"Astrid, my name is Astrid." She smiled.

SEASIDE RENDEZVOUS

by
Kristin Dearborn

The black Atlantic swirls against the rock—sometimes thrashing and pounding, sometimes so still it looks to be glass. At high tide, it devours the rockweed and the barnacles, covers the mussels and tide pools. Then it retreats, laying the sharp granite bare.

A figure picks her way through the rocks, determined, the pace never changing ... but she wobbles here and there, feet never slipping. Her ankles bend oddly as they find purchase on the slippery rock. She weaves her head from side to side, searching for something. Her clothes are tatters, bladderwort woven in among the tresses of her hair. Even though it's November, she's been outside so much the sun has bleached her hair almost blond. Her broken teeth scrape at her gums. She doesn't bleed any more. The taste of blood, even her own, would have stoked the raging fire in her. The figure, past the point of a growling stomach, thinks of nothing but food as she slips on seaweed but doesn't fall.

The birds have learned to steer clear of this place. It's strange to see a section of coastline not punctuated with bright white seagulls. If one is new it lands, surveys the area, and even while noticing the overabundance of rock crabs, it decides not to take its chances and flaps off elsewhere.

The crows are the only exception. They land on the trees high above, finding safety in numbers. The trees here are stunted and gnarled from the battering of the wind. When the crows speak to each other, she whips her head around. Deep down she knows she'll never catch them—they're not like the gulls—but she always tries. It leaves the deep hunger inside her boiling more than when she began, but the hope of catching one drives her.

Crows know, though. They pass knowledge along, generation to generation. While these crows perching in the trees haven't seen this before, they understand. They don't scavenge or hunt here, and they never drop down within arm's reach. They do check on her from time to time, the whole group descending on branches together, watching.

A seal, old and dying, brings himself up on the rocks, hoping to find warmth and dignity in his last moments. From a mile away, she catches his scent and sprints. Her sneakers are torn and tattered from the jagged shells, from muscles and barnacles, from the way the rock formed here. Sharp mica and quartz stabbing through the granite and glittering in what little light is left here in the late fall. It doesn't matter.

On the hunt, her footing becomes impeccable as she traverses her terrain. Her sweater is torn and hangs open in wide gaps, trailing woolen yarn. Underneath is Lycra long underwear, stinking of blood and a foul sweat as her body literally devours itself from the inside out. All because she can't find enough. She is *hungry*.

The seal is too tired and too slow to quite know what to make of her when she descends on him. By the time he parses out the odd scent and sees the crows startle, it's too late. He knew the two-leggeds would attack, but always they used harpoons, guns—at the very least, knives.

Her empty hands confuse him. Her madness confuses him. Her hunger sends him back to the sea, struggling to hurry over the rocks. Water is safety. His kind isn't used to predators outside the water, and he moves his bulk far too slowly.

The seal is meat and she eats until she throws up, half into the sea, half onto the rocks. A bloody mass of blubber and flesh. Then she falls on him again and eats more. So hungry. This isn't it. Isn't enough. Isn't right.

Close but no cigar, words from another time that mean nothing to her now, flit through her addled, starving brain.

She traverses the rocks now. Hoping, hungry.

One day she sees a small motorboat out in the water. The scents assault her. Gasoline, dead fish, but mostly the smell of the most amazing and delicious food she can imagine and she remembers a time when she got to enjoy it. On her hands and knees, face buried in the entrée. On the shoreline, she wails and beats at her chest, not willing to go into the dark, swirling Atlantic. Needing what's out there.

She paces the shoreline for days after the boat passes. Saliva dribbles from the corners of her mouth, and she's long past the point of wiping it away. The crows watch, passing their judgments. Finally, her rhythms come back to normal and she resumes her patrol. Traversing the rocks, whipped by the wind, driven only by a hunger that burns.

In my mouth, in my mouth, oh god it's in my mouth.

Rebecca pawed at her tongue, not caring that her hands were filthy. The taste of dirt contrasted with the oily, thick flavor of . . . whatever had just come up from the corpse's mouth. She glanced around to see who was watching, but everyone had their own work and was preoccupied. Trying to keep her mouth open, she thought for some dumb reason that exposure to air would kill the germs.

Rebecca stood, her knees popping louder than ever before. She wasn't even that old; it wasn't fair. Easier to think about creaky knees than *whatever* she'd taken into her mouth. Her stomach lurched thinking about it. Pathogens, things the world hadn't seen for hundreds of years.

In my mouth!

She hauled herself up and out of the hole they'd excavated, where the midden site was at its deepest, ancient trash from a people who'd been gone from here since the late fourteenth century or so, though they couldn't be sure till they'd dated the artefacts in the lab. Sucking in a deep breath, she forced herself to be calm, casually went to the tent where Starsha had set up cookies and bottles of water. Rebecca picked up a bottle of Poland Springs, sucked in the lukewarm water, and spat on the ground. Traces of the black ichor landed in the dry grass. It made her stomach heave. Had she swallowed any? She didn't think so.

She glanced around the site. A few hundred feet away, the Atlantic was as calm as it ever got in the afternoon, waves rhythmically drumming against the rocks. Close to the waterline, seagulls fought over the body of a large crab. In the trees, a murder of crows watched her. She shivered … it didn't seem like they watched the dig, or the seagulls, or the ocean. They watched her.

They were her only witnesses. Abernathy, the dig leader, carefully brushed dirt away from pottery scraps and mussel shells. Starsha spread out notable finds on a blue tarp, carefully cataloging each piece on her laptop. Rebecca and Brian had been working on the body. *Body* made it sound too recent. The woman had been dead a long time. They'd called the police, the medical examiner had come, spent a few minutes with them this afternoon before declaring yes, the body was archaeological; no, the police didn't need to investigate.

The rules seemed silly, but police liked to know when human remains were involved. It didn't really make sense—the state police and medical examiner weren't equipped to deal with forensic anthropology, not really. Jordan Becker was coming from the University of Maine, but they didn't expect him until next week sometime. Rebecca knew a little, but also knew these people wouldn't throw a dead woman into their garbage dump. It hadn't sat well with her from the beginning, and when she'd finally been allowed to move the almost-mummified corpse, there shouldn't have been anything *wet*.

Judging from the condition of the bones and teeth, the woman had died of starvation, but of course Becker would do a more thorough examination in the lab. She hated the idea of handing off the body to him; this was *her find*. But he was the expert, and her name would appear on his results, somewhere down with his flock of adoring grad students.

The teeth weren't right though, and that had bothered Rebecca as she moved to exhume the skull a little more carefully. That was when the bloody thing coughed on her, a spurt of black ichor, and it'd gone right inside her mouth. The site was dry, though, hadn't rained in days. Nothing here was wet. There shouldn't be anything to slosh or splash.

She checked her watch and saw that it was close to quitting time for the day. Usually it took wild horses to drag her from the site, but the idea of spending another moment here, in the pit, with that *thing*, further turned her stomach.

The dig site was in Followe's Landing, a microscopically small town on the coast of Maine, between Machias and Lubec. Residents drove miles to get to a grocery store, a gas station. There was nothing in Followe's Landing and that's the way the 200 residents liked it. There was, however, a grange hall about a half-mile along the coast from the dig site. After petitioning and permitting, three town meetings explaining the benefits of learning about the indigenous people who'd once lived on this section of coast, the town allowed the team to take up residence in their precious grange hall and use the kitchen. Rebecca trudged through the narrow path back to the hall. The rest of the team, if they drove, would cover about five miles.

The crew had set up one long table—it reminded Rebecca a little bit of the last supper, especially the way Abernathy parked in the middle and held court over the grad students—then hung some pipe-and-drape curtains, partitioning off a sleeping area. The town provided ten miserable cots for the eight of them. Starsha was smart enough to have brought one of those ridiculous giant air mattresses with its own pump.

Like on most days, when Rebecca slipped through the back door of the grange hall the mattress was mostly deflated. She dropped to her cot. She heard someone, most likely Bitters, in the kitchen preparing dinner. She felt the hard bars of the cot through the thin mattress. Alternately it made her feel like a child and a penitent. Both seemed apt.

She hadn't swallowed any of the material. If she had, she would have gone back to Brian, an anthropological medical doctor, and told him. She'd spat it all out soon enough that it was a bad memory. A funny joke, a story she'd tell in a few years. She imagined a fresh batch of baby grad students recoiling and laughing. *"Eeeew!"* Instead, shame draped her shoulders. She shouldn't have had her mouth open, shouldn't have let it happen, shouldn't have just run away when it did. There should be an accident report. Well, she'd tell Brian at dinner. Soon. Her eyes dropped closed, and a catnap never hurt anyone.

She dozed until a too-cheerful voice woke her.

"Here she is!" Starsha knelt by her cot. "Hey, are you all right?"

No, Rebecca realized upon waking up, she wasn't.

"I don't feel great. My stomach's a little off."

"Well, dinner is served. If your stomach's not feeling well, I don't see why you'd want to miss Bitters' famous sloppy joes."

Rebecca's stomach roiled and she must have made a face. Starsha frowned.

"I can see what else we've got. When I was a kid and I was sick, my mom always made me scrambled eggs. Anything sound good to you?"

Compassion, coming from Starsha the diva, made Rebecca's cheeks burn.

"No, I'm good." As an afterthought: "Thanks."

She sat up and realized she hadn't even taken her boots off. "It's not that bad. I'll go for the joes."

Starsha looked relieved, tossed her blond hair, and said, "Well, then dinner is served."

Starsha headed back through the curtained partition to the table. She was a confident young woman who led with her chest, had been a double major in theater and anthropology, and every summer vanished for three months to do outdoor Shakespeare theater. Rebecca had seen her plays. Starsha wasn't a good enough actress to break past the summer festival circuit—yet—but she was outstanding at sorting through paleolithic trash and identifying bits and pieces. Behind her back everyone always said she needed to choose, else she'd always be mediocre at both.

A pang slashed at Rebecca's stomach, and she identified it for what it was. Hunger. She was so hungry she'd moved beyond wanting to eat, and now just felt sick. She'd missed lunch, having been so engrossed with the bored medical examiner who'd had to come all the way from Bangor to tell them to keep doing what they were doing. She sat next to Brian, on the end, meaning to tell him about the black slime getting in in her mouth, but the words didn't come. The folding table legs banged into her knees no matter where she scooted her folding metal chair.

"Where'd you go?" Brian took a bite of his sandwich, viscous sloppy joes matter dripping onto his plate to punctuate the question.

Luckily Starsha was there to answer for her. "She's not feeling well. It's her stomach." Starsha tossed her an empathetic pout.

"You think you ate something with lunch?"

Rebecca thought they should all stop talking about it and focus on something else.

"How's the skeleton?" Bruce wiped his mouth.

"Perfect table talk for someone with an upset tummy." Starsha rolled her eyes.

Rebecca managed, "All tucked in for the night. Ready for another day tomorrow."

"Did you notice anything odd?"

Everything. Blackness, something that spread. She swallowed past thick saliva and made her voice sound normal. "My guess is starvation. These winters are brutal. We'll know more when Becker gets here."

Given that she'd found the skeleton in what seemed to be an indigenous midden, she'd thought it was a native. On further examination—which Becker and his lab would provide in hours—she was pretty sure it was a settler. Which didn't make sense with their timeline.

Becker would get it all straightened out, and whatever wrong information she shared would be condescendingly corrected. "You're still learning, kid!" he'd said last time they worked together. He'd squeezed her shoulder, *maybe* going for avuncular, but succeeding only in creepy.

"That's a little off for this period or region," Brian said.

Rebecca's stomach yowled with hunger, people looked at her, and she reluctantly shoveled a forkful of sloppy joes into her mouth.

Was the meat rancid?

There was something very wrong with the food. She glanced around the table, everyone making small talk, eating.

She smiled and pushed away from the table, headed directly (but not in a panic, she hoped) towards the bathroom. Closed the wooden door behind her, and immediately vomited into the toilet, trying to be as quiet as she could manage. She desperately didn't want to lose the food in her stomach, whatever remnants there were from before lunch, but up it all came, and she heaved until only yellow bile was left.

In the aftermath, her mouth tasted of the blackness that had come from the site, and she gagged again until her stomach muscles and throat protested. She rinsed her mouth with the questionable tap water. Ray, the expedition leader, had advised they not drink it, but she didn't care. She spat into the sink, ropes of normal-looking post-vomit phlegm, but no sign of the blackness.

I didn't swallow it, she reminded herself. *Didn't swallow any.*

Her stomach rumbled.

Food poisoning. Must be. She'd never had it before, so this must be it. The rational part of her mind stepped in and pointed out that a strange substance in her mouth, particularly one from a grave, and then a coincidental onset of food poisoning that didn't seem to be affecting any of the rest of the crew, didn't add up. She should tell Brian, but was there any evidence left? He wouldn't believe her if she came to him with just a story. Hell, she wouldn't believe herself. In a 400-year-old corpse in a dry burial environment it was practically impossible for there to be something wet, let alone something wet that ... jumped.

She didn't like that word or its implications so she pushed it away. It wasn't quite right anyway. She'd been face to face with the dead woman, scraping dirt from the nose and open mouth. She shouldn't have had her own mouth open. She splashed water on her face, and as subtly as she could, slipped from the bathroom behind the curtain to the sleeping quarters. She'd do something nice in the morning to clean up from dinner. Double breakfast dishes. Something extra nice. This time she kicked off her shoes before dropping onto the cot, feeling the metal supports brace against her.

The sounds of the camp went on around her. Laughing, talking, and clinking dishes and running water as the cleanup started. She strained to hear her name—had anyone even noticed she was gone? Likely not, everyone was so wrapped up in their own lives. One by one the others came through the flimsy curtain and dropped into their cots. She'd turned her back to them so it was a murmur of voices, shuffling of feet, and creaking of the small cots. They all wore shoes until they got into bed, all tracked sand into the grange hall, and by now there was so much sand on the floor a bare foot would be covered the moment it touched down. Each shoe crunched loudly in the sand.

"Air mattresses next time," someone said. Rebecca agreed.

"Too expensive. These cots have been here since World War II. Don't have to plug them in," someone else said.

"More like since the Civil War."

Muted laughter of people trying to be quiet. Rebecca debated snapping at them and accusing them of waking her up just to make them feel bad. Her stomach did the work instead, and growled loudly. She clenched her fists, trying to ignore the screaming hunger in her gut.

Everyone was quiet. Their gaze bored into Rebecca's back. She almost rolled over to confront them, but she wasn't sure it was worth it. One by one, the light of smartphones winked out. Ray was up the latest, with a little lamp and a paper book. Of course he was. Always had to be different.

When she was sure everyone else was asleep, Rebecca stepped back into her boots and slipped out as quietly as she could.

The back of the grange hall opened into a copse of pines, with a well-trodden path that led to the beach, to the dig site. She'd walked it many times in the daylight, but never like this in the dark. The tall pines blotted out most of the sky, but where they didn't it shone with a million stars. Very little light pollution interfered with their brilliance this far east. Each star was a pinprick of light shining with a cold brightness.

Her eyes had already adjusted to the darkness, and the shadows didn't bother her. The wind rustled through the tops of the trees, almost drowned out by the surf's relentless pounding of the rocks. The salt tang from the sea floated in the air. Rebecca was hungry. So hungry that tears sprang to the corners of her eyes.

Starsha was the first to notice the empty bed. It was a bit after four and the first morning brightness floated into the big room. Ray snored and her cot was uncomfortable. Starsha laced up her running shoes and readied herself for the day. She loved the work at the dig site—sea air, layers of history—but the grange hall was the most miserable place she'd stayed since she left her final crappy college apartment.

Outside, the hairs on the back of her neck stood up. It promised to be a hot day. No wind blew through the pines. The only sound was the steady drone of the surf. No birds sang her good morning.

Instinct told Starsha that maybe today wasn't such a good day for a run, to turn around and go inside. But humans aren't conditioned to listen to instincts, so Starsha popped in her earbuds, gave two tentative stretches, and took off down the trail.

A branch snapped, but Starsha never heard it. Footfalls pounded behind her, and Starsha never knew until something descended on her from behind, sending her facedown into the rock. When she tried to scream, soil and stone and pine needles filled her mouth. By then it was too late.

Her first feeding, finally something that satiated the hunger. She wasn't Rebecca anymore, the promising grad student; all pieces of who she'd been had slipped into the ether in the hours before dawn, when she'd found herself investigating the carcass of a dead seal washed up on the rocks. It was close to what she wanted, she could tell it was, but her stomach yowled and told her this wasn't it. By the time she made her way back to the grange hall, Rebecca had melted away, and only hunger remained.

A new smell had caught her attention. Light, feminine sweat, yesterday's deodorant, sunscreen, and the faint odor of a woman without regular access to a shower. Rebecca's mouth began to water, saliva running down her chin, the need building in her so frustrating tears sprang to her eyes.

Starsha was fast, but she always ran her same route. Rebecca tucked herself into the trees, and as Starsha ran past, all pink leggings and blond ponytail, Rebecca descended on her prey without any flicker of recognition. Instead of an esteemed colleague, the hunger descended on a walking meat unit, digging into the unprotected soft parts.

Screams rent the morning, but the dig team was so used to Ray's snoring that many of them used white noise machines or headphones. No one stirred, until later, when they opened the doors and the hunger came to them. Each one delicious, but none of them enough.

Now she is alone again. Each of the lives she devoured is a perfect respite—but so brief. With each meal, the hunger comes back stronger, more agonizing. The seal was down to an unsatisfying skeleton before the sea took it, tooth marks in the bones. It made her sick, it wasn't what she wanted. She couldn't process it.

Somewhere not too far from here, a car door slams. She smells the sterilization of air conditioning, expensive leather, cologne. Some kind of pomade. He smells delicious, and her excitement sends her towards him on fleet feet. Saliva slides down her chin. She will show Dr. Becker what she's found.

RED RUN

by
Querus Abuttu

"When the yellow flies cluster on the James' muddy waters, hide your sons—plug your ears against the screams of Miller's Daughters."
~Unknown Canal Man (1800s)

Bran surveyed each of the inner tubes. They were fully inflated and ready to go. She patted them approvingly.

That ought to do it. No air leaks.

Koah and Duggit sprinted by, hooting and laughing, each snatching up a tube and jumping into the river. Water splashed into the air and the flying droplets shimmered like thousands of brilliant crystals under the sun despite the river's muddiness. It had rained like hell last night and the swirling brown of the James wasn't something people usually went tubing in.

Bran's eyes followed and then lingered on Koah. She was hypnotized by his tan skin and near-perfect body. She inhaled the newly washed air. After a hard rain, the air seemed fresh and pure, as if nature had just run the world through a giant wash-and-rinse cycle. She breathed in deeply once more, letting the scents of honeysuckle and wet earth fill her nose and recharge her insides.

Gazing upward, she admired the glorious turquoise color above her. The sky was that kind of hue that easily mesmerized a person—captured their fascination so much they just wanted to stare—to fall into it forever. A dull rushing of water pulled her gaze back to the river.

The river today was the direct opposite of the sky. It roiled, swift and angry, and it smelled of decaying trees and leaves. A dead fish floated by and then the ripples of current sucked it under. the ripples of current.

Bran's stomach knotted as she stared at the water. Something about it didn't feel right. And it didn't feel smart, going tubing today. She thought about calling out to Koah and Duggit.

Maybe I can convince them to come back—call off the trip . . .

"Brandon!"

The sound came from behind her, and Bran could have picked out that voice in a heavy-metal concert crowd. The baritone had a raspy rumble that reminded her of the very first earthquake she'd ever experienced.

She turned to see Joe lumbering toward her. He was always the man with the plan. When they were bored and hanging out inside, he found shit for them to do when the rest of them were too lazy to come up with something cool. Any video game was toast if he walked into the room. If it weren't for him, they'd probably never go outside. He slapped Bran on the back and gave her a half-hug, his flaming red beard blowing against her ear. She brushed the hair away from her face.

"Dude! Just got back. Dropped off our truck at Colombia. Mr. Morrow brought me back," he said. "Our wheels are all set, ready to ride soon as we pull in."

Columbia was just a few miles away by river. The town was once a major hub of business before the Civil War. Now, the population totaled less than one hundred people, and the dilapidated houses were testimony to the long-term effects of hurricanes Camille and Agnes that nearly wiped it from the map.

Bran tried to sound excited. "Dealio!" She gave him a double thumbs-up, glad he'd called her "dude," which meant she was still one of the guys.

It wasn't easy for her to grow up as a girl named Brandon. Adults in Iron Shores had often called her a tomboy. She remembered some of the local women bringing her hand-me-down dresses when she was in her teens. A subtle hint that she should dress more like a girl. Perhaps a more obvious hint she should act more like a girl.

Despite all that, she liked her name. Her father had named her Brandon because, well, he'd wanted a boy. Her family tried to cutesify it and call her Brandy, but she hated that name with a passion and always let them know. It never made a speck of difference.

And even though she liked guy things, she wasn't a dyke or a lesbian or whatever people might wonder. Not that she was against same-sex relationships, because she had several friends who were gay. No, she just preferred guys even though she always gravitated toward boy's, and now men's, stuff. She liked their clothing, genuinely enjoyed football, and loved to play a scrimmage in backyard games.

Bran was also the kind of girl who loved working on cars. High-end muscle cars were her favorite. Her college major was criminal justice. She wanted a career in law enforcement or something similar. Officer Luck, one of two town badges, always told her great stories. It was better than gossip because his info was official. She knew more about the families and the crimes committed in Iron Shores than almost anyone.

Unfortunately, she was also the first to be overlooked when it came to finding a potential mate. Most men, she discovered, wanted calendar women—the kind of girls with soft gooey eyes and large breasts. Women who did macho activities with their men but weren't quite as good at it.

Bran was five feet ten inches, nearly flat chested, and did things better than most guys she knew. She wore her dark hair short in the back and long in the front, and although she wasn't extremely strong, she was wiry, toned, and fast on her feet. Faster than most of her friends.

Bran's gaze swept over the banks of the river. Underneath the dappled leaves of cottonwoods, the yellow flies clustered in large, thick groups, floating on top of the water like a rippling blanket of monochrome wings and golden bodies. This was how they bred—in muddy water.

"Joe. Dude, you really think we should be going?" She gestured toward the river and the yellow flies. "Remember what they told us in Webelos?"

Yes, Bran was once a Webelo. And yes, the cubmaster, old Mr. Ressler, still thought she was a guy to this day.

Joe gave her a blank stare and shook his head.

She hiked her eyebrows up for emphasis. "Beware the Miller's Daughters?"

The old saying had merit when it came to this part of the James. People had died or disappeared more than once on the river, and most often after a hard rain.

"Yeah, and you still believe in Santa and the Easter Bunny too?" Joe chuckled and threw her a vest.

Bran never had the chance to believe in Santa or anything like him. Her parents, die-hard scientists, had squashed those bugs long ago, feeling it was wrong to tell kids about things that didn't exist. But she knew from experience that there were unexplainable things that *did* exist.

One night in particular Bran remembered waking up to find a Native American woman at the foot of her bed staring straight at her with piercing eyes. The woman was wrapped in a striped blanket, and her long black hair was plaited to one side. Bran had panicked, but was unable to move. She tried calling for help, but her voice didn't work. After what seemed like forever, her muscles finally obeyed her brain. When she sat up and blinked, she was startled to find the woman was gone. Her parents chided her. Said it was sleep paralysis.

Later, she asked her friend Renny about what she saw. Renny was a descendant of the Monacan tribe. She and her family owned the town's used bookstore.

"You went hiking the day before?" Renny asked her.

"Yeah," Bran said, "but what's that got to do with it?"

"Where'd you go hiking?"

Bran thought the question was crazy.

"Hazard's Creek. Why?"

"You bring your shoes inside the house?" The woman eyed her while she put some books away.

"Well, yeah. Who doesn't?"

Renny nodded. "Then there's your problem. Hazard's got an old Native burial ground near those trails. If you wandered off the path, you probably passed through there. Our people believe if a person walks over a burial ground, and then they bring their shoes inside, they invite the spirits into their home. The spirits aren't always friendly."

"No way." Bran had never heard of such a thing.

"Way. Clean your shoes," Renny advised. "Smudge them and your house with the smoke from burning cedar leaves. Light the leaves like incense, and blow the fire out so just the red embers let the smoke rise up. Fan it out with a feather. And—don't ever go hiking there again."

That was just one of the things Bran had experienced in her life that was unexplainable—one of the things that stretched far beyond facts and far outside the realm of what people called science. And that's why she knew the Miller's Daughters legend was not a joke. Bran's cousin Jude hadn't listened after a particularly hard rain the night before he'd gone out with friends on a canoe trip last year. Near the old town of Passage his body was found broken on the rocks, his head smashed in, just along the shores of the old mill. They never found his friends.

Bran put on her life vest, still feeling sick in the pit her stomach. She knew they shouldn't go, but everyone was so psyched, and it was their last day to be together before school started and they went their separate ways.

Koah waved at her. "We're leaving without you, dude. C'mon!" He flashed that Colgate smile Bran worked so hard not to fall in love with. Resistance was futile, because her heart skipped a beat. She couldn't not go.

Duggit, the group's gentle giant, was built like a linebacker, but of all things he was an artist. He used his thick hands for making pottery. Much of it intricate, light and delicate. A sharp contrast to the man who did the crafting.

Duggit grinned back at her. The Dallas ball cap he never went anywhere without crowned the loose brown curls of his head. His inner tube was the largest of them all. Sixty-eight inches—the biggest they could find.

Maybe there's really nothing to worry about. Her thoughts were far from convincing.

Bran licked her lips and ran her teeth over them. Mr. Kessler's words about the river looped in her brain.

When the yellow flies cluster on the James' muddy waters, hide your sons—plug your ears against the screams of Miller's Daughters.

Bran shook her head and stuck the cooler of beer in the center of a tube. She grabbed up the rope and tied the tube to her own.

Nothing. Just a saying. A worn-out ghost story passed down through the decades.

The Miller's Daughters. Again, she heard the echo of old man Ressler's stories. Back in the 1800s, the mill took in deliveries from batteau on the Kanawha canals, which ran parallel to the James. They transported city goods like cloth and fine china upriver, and returned to the cities with farmed goods like grains and produce.

During the Civil War, Union soldiers burned down the mill. When the town miller rebuilt it, sparks from the new train—which replaced the canals ten years later—burnt it down again. The mill wasn't resurrected after that, and the town—it simply died.

Legend was, part of the river was haunted with the angry spirits of girls the Union Army had raped and killed when they marched though. No one knew for sure because no one had ever seen the spirits or verified the tale. But every now and again someone found a body on the river rocks near the remains of the mill.

Old man Ressler was adamant, saying never to get on the river when it was muddy. He'd taught land survival in Webelos for years.

"If you see yellow flies along the banks, you wait," he said. "The river has her ways in these parts, and she'll sing to you, entice you. But never go in when the water isn't clear. You wait, you hear?"

Mr. Ressler had always called the river "she." And when the river water wasn't clear, he never went near it. Bran often wondered if there was a link between Mr. Ressler's deadly river and his tale of the Miller's Daughters. Were they one and the same?

Bran stuffed her reluctance into the pit of her queasy belly and cast off. Before long the four of them were swirling down the river. Because of the muddy water, they had no clue what was below them, and the current was moving fast enough that if they didn't pay attention they'd run onto the rocks or get snagged on fallen tree branches.

The guys didn't seem to mind. They laughed as they floated and carried on. Bran threw beers out to everyone. They popped the tops, guzzled some suds, and cracked raunchy jokes. Every now and then, she thought she saw a face rise in the rushing water, rivulets of hair twisting in the whirlpools of the current. Then she'd look hard and the vision faded away.

I'm imagining things. Letting the stories get to me.

About twenty minutes into their ride, both of Bran's ears started itching. It was like something irritating trying to crawl inside. Then, a high-pitched whine in her head. She spied the crumbling rock wall of the ruined mill on the left, near the remains of the old canals. They were close to the town of Passage. A place the forest had swallowed whole after everyone left.

Her gaze pivoted over to Duggit and Koah. They were rubbing their ears too. The river swirled and reshaped right in front of them and Bran did a double take. The muddy current undulated and two tan mounds rose upward, looking all the world like enormous breasts. And Joe and Duggit's tubes were headed straight for them.

Bran's stomach lurched.

"Joe, no! Duggit! Stay away!" The water roared over her yell. "Koah!"

Koah turned his head. His eyes were unfocused, glazed over as if he were in some kind of trance. He swiveled back toward to the watery mounds.

It's the sound! Some connection with the itching and the whine.

Bran fished a folding knife from the pocket of her shorts and cut a couple of strips from her shirt. She rolled them into balls and pushed them into her ears. She tore a couple more strips, pulled herself out of her tube and swam hard to catch Koah. Grabbing him by the shirt, she stuffed the wads into his ears. It was all she had. All she could think to do. She watched her tube and the cooler of beer speed by without her.

A sudden gust of wind rose up and pushed against all of them, their tubes lurching forward from the force. Joe and Duggit swirled away from her faster and faster. Duggit's cap, caught by the wind, flew off and spun into the trees. He didn't even seem to notice.

The guys reached the watery breasts and stuck their hands out as if to stroke them. Thick ropes of water, big around as a bodybuilder's arms, stretched toward the men as if anticipating some insane embrace.

Bran paddled toward them, towing Koah, yelling, "Stop!" Her attempt to warn them died in her throat when she watched the watery arms grab Joe and Duggit. The water ran along their bodies in a sensual caress and both men's faces were clothed in a strange mask of ecstasy. Then, as quickly as the water had wrapped them in an aquatic embrace, the arms raised them high into the air and dashed their bodies against the jutting rocks. The water bore them up again and struck them once more against the jagged edges of stone, splitting both of their skulls wide open.

The tan breasts and aqueous arms churned, turning red, almost as if the river were receiving some sort of macabre transfusion. Bran was frozen, her mouth open, her next scream dead on her lips. She stared into the water. Were those—baby faces? They were distorted, twisted—forming, dissolving, and then reforming. She thought of the yellow flies.

This thing, whatever it is—is it breeding? Like horseflies, did it need a blood meal? No. That's crazy. Fucking insane.

Bran and Koah had almost reached the area where Joe and Duggit had been smashed. Bran couldn't touch bottom. She yelled to Koah, but he couldn't hear her now. He stared forward, fixated on the scene before him.

Bloody-red baby faces surrounded the watery breasts. Their mouths opened wide, revealing an abyss of black—a horrible dread-filling darkness. The muddy appendages reached out again, splitting into fine tendrils. Bran watched with incredulity as they reached Koah's ears and plucked the cloth wads out.

No! No!

"You can't have him!" she screamed at the river. "He's mine!"

The bulging, tan breasts jiggled and undulated as if the water was laughing. The baby heads turned tan and melted into the rapids.

Bran attempted to duck under the edge of Koah's inner tube so she could climb up into it with him, but then he slipped from the tube's center and into the river. She managed to grab his arm, pull him close and clutched him tightly to her chest. Together they tumbled in the rushing waters, but their life vests kept them afloat. She wrapped her legs around him and tried hard to cover his ears with her hands.

Then he kissed her. His lips were warm and full. His body, hard and lean. Bran's skin flushed with warmth and, although she knew in the back of her mind that they'd just witnessed their friends dying at the hands of whatever it was in the river, she was suddenly overtaken by an insatiable physical need for him.

Bran touched her hands to her ears. Her makeshift earplugs were gone. The river's song, sweet and succulent, was no longer just a high-pitched whine. It filled her head and her body. She felt an intense rush of heat. Her groin tingled and she felt wet and electric all at the same time.

What the hell's the matter with me?

But it was Koah—Koah who reached for her, who kissed her again and who she kissed back with an insatiable passion that drove her onward with a fury.

"I want you," he said, his husky voice barely audible over the rushing water.

"Then take me," she murmured into his ear.

She was rocked with a wild abandon so uncharacteristic of her pensive ways. She didn't care what the world saw, or what anyone thought. She didn't care about right or wrong. All she could think of was how much she wanted to be with Koah—how much she wanted to absorb every fiber of him and have him to herself.

They swam to the shore, rolling with each other in the waters until their feet touched bottom. Bran quickly stripped him from his vest and he roughly removed hers. They tugged each other's shirts from their bodies, and shed their shorts on the river bank.

She gazed at him in one long, lust-filled moment, and lay down on the sand. Koah followed her, his bare chest covering hers, rubbing against her breasts. She arched against him and wrapped her legs around his waist, gasping as his pushed into her. The sharp pain disappeared almost as soon as she felt it, and then there was the delicious sensation of him moving inside her, thrusting into her.

In the full waves of pleasure, they rutted in the sand, feeling the ebb and flow of life in their motions. Bran arched as the warmth from him pumped into her body and together they slowed like a ripple gradually fading across the face of a still pond. Afterwards, panting, they curled against each other in languid repose.

"I always wondered what it would be like," he murmured. "Being with you. I'm yours, Bran, now and forever." He closed his eyes, his breath soon rising and falling in waves of heavy sleep.

Again, the song rippled across the water and enveloped her like a cozy blanket of sound. It filled her like Koah had filled her minutes ago.

I should stop. I should run.

And she tried. She really did. But something about the primordial water, its song and the wild abandon she'd shared with Koah—something in the feeling warmed her, pressed into her, and suddenly she wanted more.

Take him, the river song whispered in her ears. *Make him a part of you. For always.*

Bran closed her eyes. Knew what she had to do. She rolled Koah onto the ground and grabbed him by his hair. Odd, he didn't fight. And she wasn't surprised that he didn't feel heavy.

She easily dragged him back into the river, his body limp from lovemaking and unawakenable sleep. Cradling his head in her hands, she pressed her lips against his and pushed her tongue into his mouth, giving him a lust-filled kiss that made her blood rush faster, her body feel hotter. She heard him murmur, "Yours. Forever."

And then she smiled, knowing they were free. Her legs straddled his hips and she felt him slip inside her once again. She ground against him and rode his body as her fingers reached around his throat and squeezed hard until his eyes rolled back and turned white—and then pleasure wracked her body as her pelvic muscles contracted in rapid spasms that gradually slowed into gentle waves of bliss.

She kissed his lips, cooler now, and then dragged him to the center of the river, near some of the rocks jutting up from the water. The water caressed their bodies. Moved sensuously between her thighs. Watery breasts rose up again, and beautiful faces swirled around her.

Do it. Now. Become one.

With a scream that came from the roots of ancient forests, from the furious white rapids born anew every second, she hauled Koah up over her head, strength surging from some unknown chasm of her body, and throwing him down, she broke his skull open wide against the jagged rocks.

Bran pursed her lips, and crouched down next to him. She cupped her hands, enjoying the feel of his warm blood pooling into her palms. Bringing her hands to her mouth, she gulped down his energy in a glorious red feeding that somehow she knew would bring forth new life and let her morph with the Mother River, with all of nature, forever.

Five weeks had passed since two fishermen discovered Bran on the banks of the river James, naked and shivering, somewhere near Columbia. Her three friends were never found. Iron Shores law enforcement visited when she got home. Officers Ware and Luck tried to be respectful, but Bran could tell they suspected she knew more than she was saying.

"And you still don't remember what happened?" Officer Ware's somber gray eyes focused on her intently.

Bran shrugged and shook her head. "Not a thing. One minute we were floating down the river, laughing, drinking beers. The next, someone is putting me into an ambulance."

The officers finished up their questions and left the house. Once they were gone, Bran went into the bathroom and did two things. First, she vomited up her lunch—a peanut butter and jelly sandwich. She wouldn't eat peanut-butter for at least two years after that. Next, she peed on a stick and read the results.

She already had baby names picked out for a girl or a boy. Other than that, she didn't know what else to do. Maybe go back to school and make up the work she'd missed. Maybe figure out how to be a single mom. She'd scrape by until the summer—until the rains poured down and the yellow flies bred once more. And then, when the Miller's Daughters sang their songs, she'd feed.

AUTHOR, EDITOR AND ARTIST BIOS

Querus Abuttu, "Dr. Q.," is an award-winning author and U.S. Navy veteran. She earned an MFA from Seton Hill University in 2014 and writes dark tales that often center around environmental destruction and various forms of violence. She works as a writer, anthologist, and editor at Scary Dairy Press. Dr. Q. is the author of the novel *Sapient Farm*, and has had several short stories published in anthologies like *Mother's Revenge, Terror Politico* and *Hazard Yet Forward*. She lives in the wilds of Virginia where she hunts down feral phantoms and makes their stories her own. Free stories are on her website at Querus-Abuttu.com Follow Dr. Q. on Twitter @Querus_Abuttu, on Instagram at https://www.instagram.com/querusabuttu/ and on her Facebook Author page at DrQAbuttu. Her author page on Amazon lists many of her publications:
https://www.amazon.com/Querus-Abuttu/e/B009NDJ2RM

Amber Bliss's quest for stories started in childhood and continued to Seton Hill University, where she earned her MFA in writing popular fiction. She works in Rhode Island as a librarian, and through a supportive community and a little sorcery she's managed to combine her love of writing, stories, and tabletop roleplaying games into her day job. She is owned by one cat and way too many D&D campaigns. Follow her on twitter @am_bliss or visit her website www.amberbliss.com

Sally Bosco writes horror and young adult fiction. She's inexplicably drawn to the uncanny, the shades of gray between the light and dark, the area where your mind hovers as you're falling off to sleep. She graduated from the University of Florida with a BA in graphic design and has an MFA in writing popular fiction from Seton Hill University. Her longer works include the novels *Death Divided, The Werecat Chronicles*, *Shadow Cat* (written as Zoe LaPage) *Cevin's Deadly Sin*, and a novella, *Double Crush*. Other publications include a chapter in *Many Genres, One Craft* and stories in *Small Bites*, *Hazard Yet Forward* , and *Cellar Door* anthologies. Connect with her through her through Facebook, Twitter, and sallybosco.com.

Christe M. Callabro plays many roles in her life, including writer, editor, massage therapist, bellydancer, gamer, and corgi mom. She earned her MA in 2005 and her MFA in 2015 in writing popular fiction from Seton Hill University. Other published works include stories in the anthologies *Cloaked in Shadow* and *Modern Magic*, both published by Fantasist Enterprises. She lives in eastern Tennessee, which is nowhere near Graceland.

Broos Campbell has written or edited more than a dozen books, including (with Cin Ferguson) two previous anthologies for Scary Dairy Press, and has a particular interest in ships and the supernatural. His Matty Graves novels concern the triumphs and disasters of a mixed-race American officer during the early years of the U.S. Navy, but his current project is about a girl who's looking for her mother's corpse. He likes *The New Yorker* cartoons and almost laughed at one once. Look him up. He's easy to find.

Elsa M. Carruthers is a poet, writer, and independent genre scholar. She is the editor of a forthcoming collection of critical essays, *Westworld: Manufactured Humanities, Dreams, and Nightmares*. Her fiction and poetry has been published in several anthologies and magazines. Her author page on Amazon lists some of her most well-known publications:
https://www.amazon.com/Elsa-Carruthers/e/B00TKU99KS/
You can find her on Facebook at:
https://www.facebook.com/elsamcarruthersauthor/
and on Goodreads at:
https://www.goodreads.com/author/show/6476466.Elsa_M_Carruthers

Kristin Dearborn: If it screams, squelches, or bleeds, Kristin Dearborn has probably written about it. A lifelong New Englander, she aspires to follow in the footsteps of the local masters, Messrs. King and Lovecraft. When not writing or rotting her brain with cheesy horror flicks (preferably creature features!) she can be found scaling rock cliffs. zipping around Vermont on a motorcycle, or gallivanting around the globe. Kristin is the author of many short stories, three novellas, and two novels. Visit her online at www.kristindearborn.com.

Leadie Jo Flowers is the author of novels, short stories, and poetry in the genres of science fiction and horror. She makes extra money for traveling by teaching English in Moscow, Russia. She is a member of the Horror Writer's Association and you can usually find her at Stokercon, World Science Fiction, and Eurocon conferences as well as a few others. Her poetry has appeared in HWA Poetry Showcase Volume IV, and a short story in the *Hazard Yet Forward* and *Terror Politico* anthologies. You can follow what is happening with her writing at these links:
https://www.leadiejoflowers.net/
https://www.facebook.com/Leadie-Jo-Flowers-198085643573595/

Kerri-Leigh Grady is a software developer, perpetual student, terrible archer, lame BJJ white belt, lover of "ghost investigation" shows with lots of screaming and running, awful silversmith, and obsessive list maker.

Nikki Hopeman still has a trunk full of spiral-bound notebooks stuffed with short stories in a child's handwriting. While she's graduated to using a computer for writing, she still finds files of mysterious and terrifying information saved for future writing endeavors and can even sometimes remember why she saved them. In her life before writing, she earned a BS in microbiology from the University of Pittsburgh and worked as a mad scientist for the Pittsburgh Cancer Institute. She holds a master of fine arts degree in writing popular fiction from Seton Hill University, where she learned her trade with some of the best horror writers in the business. She lives in the Pittsburgh area with her husband, two sons, three corgis, and a flock of chickens. Check out her novel *Habeas Corpse*, available from Blood Bound Books on Amazon and Barnes & Noble. Also, be sure to check out her short stories, "Black Bird," in Dark Moon Books' anthology *Mistresses of the Macabre*, and "One Man's Garbage," in *Hazard Yet Forward*, a charity compilation, also available on Amazon.

Serena Jayne received her MFA in writing popular fiction from Seton Hill University. Before becoming a writer, she worked as a research scientist, a fish stick slinger, a chat wrangler, and a race horse narc. When she isn't trolling art museums for works that move her, she enjoys writing in multiple fiction genres. Her short fiction and poetry has appeared in *Switchblade Magazine*, *Crack the Spine Literary Magazine*, *the Oddville Press* and other publications.
serenajayne.com; Twitter: @SJWriter; Instagram: @jayneserenawriter
Facebook: www.facebook.com/SerenaJayneWriter/

EV Knight writes horror and dark fiction. Her debut novel, *The Fourth Whore*, will be published in 2020 by Raw Dog Screaming Press. EV's short stories can be found in *Siren's Call* magazine. A graduate of Seton Hill University, she received her MFA in writing popular fiction in January 2019. She enjoys all things macabre, whether they be film, TV, podcast, novel, or short story. She lives in the cold northern woods of Michigan's Upper Peninsula with her family and their two hairless cats.

Michelle R. Lane writes dark speculative fiction about women of color who battle their inner demons while falling in love with monsters. Her work includes elements of fantasy, horror, romance, and occasionally erotica. In January 2015, Michelle graduated with an MFA in writing popular fiction from Seton Hill University. Her short fiction appears in the anthologies *Dark Holidays* and *Terror Politico:*

A Screaming World in Chaos. Her debut novel, *Invisible Chains*, is available from Haverhill House Publishing July 2019. She lives in south-central Pennsylvania with her son.

Jennifer Loring's short fiction has been published widely both online and in print, including *Tales from the Lake vols. 1 and 4, Nightscript vol. 4*, and the upcoming anthologies *Would but Time Await: An Anthology of New England Folk Horror* and *Not All Monsters.* Longer work includes the novel *Those of My Kind* from Omnium Gatherum and the novella *Conduits* from LVP Publications. She holds an MFA in writing popular fiction with a concentration in horror fiction and teaches online in Southern New Hampshire University's College of Continuing Education. Jenn lives with her husband in Philadelphia, where they are owned by a turtle and two basset hounds. Find her online at http://jennifertloring.com

Donna J. W. Munro has spent the last twenty years teaching high school social studies. Her students inspire her every day. She has an MA in writing popular fiction from Seton Hill Writing University. Her pieces are published in *Dark Moon Digest* #34, *Syntax and Salt*, *Sirens Ezine*, *The Haunted Traveler*, *Flash Fiction Magazine*, *Astounding Outpost*, *Door=Jar*, *Spectators and Spooks Magazine*, *Nothing's Sacred Magazine* IV and V, *Hazard Yet Forward* (2012), *Enter the Apocalypse* (2017), *Killing It Softly 2* (2017), *Beautiful Lies, Painful Truths II* (2018), *Terror Politico* (2019), and several Thirteen O'Clock Press anthologies. Contact her at www.donnajwmunro.com

Mario Zucarello is an illustrator, character designer, and cartoonist. From a young age, Mario primarily taught himself the intricacies of art. After graduating from high school, he trained professionally at various Italian animation companies. Since 2007, he has been a freelance artist creating a variety of images from cartoons and humoristic pieces to high fantasy and horror. Mario's latest work, a book titled

Light and Shadows: Through the Territories of the Imaginary, will be available on Amazon in 2019. Feel free to journey to his website where you can dive right into his fantastical world: http://zuccarelloartworks.daportfolio.com/

Made in the USA
Lexington, KY
02 December 2019

57942085R00129